MAX

JULIE CAPULET

I notice him as soon as he walks into my chic new Los Angeles restaurant. Of course I do. He's tall and built, with tattoos and a dark, pirate-king vibe. According to rumors, he's also an investment genius who happens to be a billionaire.

But this is no fairy tale. He's wearing one of those criminal cuffs on one wrist and a Rolex on the other.

Just what I don't need. A rich bad boy with rage issues. It's scary enough that one of my customers has been stalking me.

But when the stalker follows me home one night, it's Max who saves me—the gorgeous blue-eyed stranger who could be either the devil or a saint.

He's dangerous, but I've never felt so safe. He's a sinner who saves me in every possible way. He becomes my haven, my protector, my paradox.

And he's the love story I never saw coming...

Max is a spin-off from the I Love You series and is a sexy standalone story.

MAX

1

I'VE HELD BACK my rage for a long time but today I feel like pummeling someone—anyone—into next goddamn week. When I find out who screwed me over…I just hope I can control myself long enough not to kill the fucker and end up in a goddamn jail cell. Then again, getting convicted for a crime I actually *did* commit might be a whole lot more satisfying than getting burned for one I didn't.

I walk through the door of my penthouse office and shut the door. What I feel like doing is slamming it, smashing the place up and hunting down the asshole who put me in this mess. But those days are long gone. I'm not an amped-up punk anymore. I'm a level-headed over-achiever with an Ivy League degree under my belt, five luxury properties to my name and a net worth of more than four hundred million dollars. I am—*was*, until earlier this afternoon—CFO of a Fortune 500 investment company and Chairman of the Goddamn Board of Directors.

I make a point of keeping my cool.

Barely.

I run a hand through my hair. I need a haircut. Hell, maybe I won't even bother. I won't be seeing the inside of a boardroom anytime soon. I stuff my $5,000 Armani jacket into one of the cardboard boxes now sitting in my office. Usually I don't show my tats at work but who gives a fuck? Today it doesn't matter. I roll up my sleeves and yank off my tie. My shirt feels too tight, possibly because I've been working out like a goddamn maniac lately. I start packing a few things from the shelves into the boxes.

My phone rings.

I almost don't answer it, but my brother's name flashes up on the screen. We have a deal: we always answer. No matter how shitty our day might've been. And today pretty much takes the cake.

Rafe launches straight into it. "Home detention's no reason to bail on me. Come out to dinner with us tonight."

"No. I'll see you tomorrow."

"Max," he says. "I'm getting *married* in two days. I need my best man there tonight to help me celebrate. Besides, Lexi found a place that's right around the corner from your office. We're heading down there now to meet Lexi's maid of honor, Tess. You met her the other night."

I got convicted of insider trading today and my brother bailed me out on the spot. Instead of a jail sentence, I'll be serving a three-month stint of home detention. I've been fitted with an electronic bracelet which, if I happen to step outside my jurisdiction, will blow my fucking head off. Okay, maybe it won't. But it might as well. I've been ordered by the judge not to leave the three-block square where my apartment and my office are located. I can walk between the two, or drive my Ducati, or any of the other six cars or twelve motorcycles parked in my private garage. If I get caught outside the zone I'll get thrown in jail for at least three years with no possibility of parole. I've also been "asked" by the Board of Directors to take a break from my job as CFO of my brother's largest investment company.

I don't really feel like dinner but, hell, I owe him one. In fact I owe him a lot more than one. Six fucking million, to be exact. "Shit. All right," I say.

The only reason I'm agreeing to meet my brother and his fiancée is because they're about to get married. I want to see them. But I wish it could be the three of us and not a foursome with some over-eager friend who's guaranteed to drool over me all night. I'm really not in the mood.

I haven't been in the mood for a while.

"I didn't do it, by the way," I say. "And I'll deposit the six mil into your Bahamas account later tonight."

"Didn't do what?"

"Leak the info."

"What do you mean?"

"I mean someone framed me." I could have told him before but there was no point. There's zero evidence to back up my claims. A stack of emails written from my private account was presented to the court, making an airtight case against me. "Someone hacked into my account and sent the emails. I didn't give out any insider information. I'm clean as a goddamn whistle."

Rafe's silent for a couple of seconds, like he can't believe what he's hearing. "Why didn't you tell me this?"

"Because I knew I didn't stand a chance in court. And I didn't want to draw it out." I have a long list of criminal offenses. Mostly minor shit I did when I was younger. Even though I've spent the past ten years trying to make up for all that by working my ass off and heading several major companies, I have enough of a record to skew any judge's opinion of me in the wrong direction. I know what I look like to a judge: a badass. A shady delinquent with a history. The kind of guy the law has a problem with.

Rafe knows all this.

"I have a few ideas about who might've framed me," I tell him, "but there's no point naming names until I have proof."

"You should've told me," Rafe says again.

"I didn't want it to look like we were trying to cover something up. Then the whole company looks dirty. This way, it's just me."

"Jesus, Max."

When you're dealing with the kind of money we throw around on a daily basis, it's dog-eat-dog, everyone knows that. I earn ten million dollars a year working for my brother, plus commission, which is usually double my salary, and sometimes more. Everyone who works with me wants my job and they all think the only reason I'm here is because my brother owns the company. Which used to be true. Not anymore. I'm good at building companies and I'm good at making money. It took me a while to get on track in life but these days I can spot a winner from a mile away.

"Until then," I add, "I'll be taking a little hiatus from the office."

"I own the damn company, Max. If you want to stay you can stay."

"I can still advise the brokers from my home office. Don't sweat it. I need a break anyway."

"I'll fucking slam whoever did this."

"Yeah, you and me both."

"I'll call an investigator I use," Rafe says. "We'll get to the bottom of this."

Taking time out from my job doesn't worry me. Letting my brother down does. Those days are over.

His sigh is pissed-off. "At least let me buy you a drink."

"Fine, then. I'll see you in twenty." I end the call and set the phone on my desk, which is strewn with court orders and legal documents. Irate letters from clients questioning my ethics and calling for my dismissal.

I'll clear my name if it's the last thing I do. I swore a long time ago I'd never get another criminal conviction, so this one stings a lot more than I'd like to admit.

I pick up a pink envelope from my stack of mail. *Another one?* Hell, she just won't quit. I get a lot of cards and letters from women. This one is from a girl I had dinner around six months ago. Or was it longer than that? I met her at a charity function, I remember that much. I'd donated a lot of money to a charity that helps down-and-out teens get into college. I *was* a down-and-out teen once so I understand how much of a difference the help of one person can make. So they sent me a free ticket to the event and I'd ended up going. She saw me from across the room and confessed she moved the seating arrangement so she could sit next to me. This happens to me all the time so I didn't think much of it. The conversation had been almost entirely one-sided. She drank a lot and asked me back to her place. Even though she was sending all the wrong signals—overly needy, borderline stalkerish, the kind of woman who clings when it's the very last thing you want them to do—I'd taken her home.

A terrible decision, as it turned out, like so many are.

It had played out the way it always does. For me, it was unfulfilling because no emotion or genuine interest was involved at all. She'd told me it was the best sex of her life, begged me to stay, then had a dramatic meltdown when I tried to leave. I hadn't called or given her my number but she knows where I work and keeps sending me letters about how I broke her goddamn heart. I had to tell the door people to stop her from entering the building after she stormed up to my office once when I was in the middle of a meeting, crying and telling me she loves me.

After *one* night. Which is crazy.

Even so, it happens all the time. Go figure.

I'm probably the least lovable person I know. I'm broken, and unfixable.

I rip open the envelope.

Max, please call me. Please!!! I need to see you one more time. I know I'll be able to change your mind. I just want to talk to you. We're meant to be together. It's destiny, I can feel it. Please let me show you how much you mean to me. Please, Max. Call me back. All my love, Melanie.

I toss the card into the shredder.

I've tried to feel that spark. I *want* to feel that spark. The one that means you're supposed to be with someone for more than one night. Maybe even for—I don't know —a *month*, maybe. Or even a whole goddamn lifetime. People *do* that shit.

The problem is, I never feel that spark and I always end up regretting everything.

So I made a decision. Probably around six months ago. Soon after Melanie, as it turns out. I decided to take a break. It's the reason I've been pumping iron like it's going out of style. All that pent up energy has to be spent somehow.

My pent up energy is on overdrive at this point. I feel like I'm about to fucking spontaneously combust.

And I'm getting tired of being alone.

It's possibly what I deserve, after the way I've treated women. Dismissive. Disengaged. Non-committal to the extreme. They accuse me of using them, then walking away. Which is true enough.

Anyway, there's no point crying about it but I'm a lost cause as far as relationships go. I came to terms with all that a long time ago.

I leave a note for my assistants to finish packing up my stuff and have it sent to my apartment. I close up my office and grab my worn black leather jacket. I walk down to the street. It's a warm night for October. There are a lot of people strolling around.

Even women who are arm-in-arm with their boyfriends or husbands check me out as I walk past.

I don't get it.

Women love me, for some reason.

Love me.

I don't dwell on it but it's just one of those things.

I've sometimes wondered what it is about me they're so desperate to have. They seem to love my looks, for better or for worse. I'm built. I'm tall. And I have an edge, which is roughly equivalent to crack for women, fuck knows why.

They even wanted me before I had money. Now, they're practically rabid.

Maybe I have the aura of someone who can do things to them no one else will. Or take them past some pleasure threshold no one else can. Who knows. Whatever it is, they watch me. They call me and pursue me relentlessly, which, lately, I've been doing my best to avoid.

I know what all this sounds like: I'm ungrateful or I'm an arrogant prick.

Not exactly.

I catch up to Rafe and Lexi just as Lexi's friend Tess is arriving, as they're walking into the restaurant. Rafe slings his arm around me like he's happy to see me. He's always happy to see me. We have the kind of bond a lot of brothers don't have. We've been through a lot together, me and him, and we know we've got each other's backs. The truth is, he's bailed me out more times than I can count but I feel like that'll start to change.

Lexi gives me a hug. My brother's fiancée is a catch, no doubt about it. She's gorgeous and is one of the nicest people I've ever met. "Hey, sweetheart," I say as she kisses my cheek. I laugh when Rafe eyeballs me. He's got some control issues when it comes to Lexi but we're cool.

The friend, Tess, who I've met once before, does what they all do: checks me out. Stares. First at my face then my body. She moves to step forward but I read her intention and take a step back before she even notices. It's something I'm well-practiced at. I don't like to be touched.

"Thanks for venturing into my jurisdiction," I say.

"For you?" Tess blushes. "Anything."

I return the smile but I'm so not in the mood for this. My muscles are clenched for no particular reason. Possibly because I'm still wound up from getting convicted of a federal offense a few hours ago and escaping a prolonged prison sentence by the skin of my goddamn teeth and six million dollars.

"Tess, let's go sit down," Lexi says, thankfully steering Tess away. I exhale, releasing a minuscule shred of the ocean of tension and despair that hounds me.

We walk further into the restaurant. "This place is so cute," Tess says.

I guess it is. It's got a lot of exposed brick and wood and mirrors. The ceiling's been decorated with yellow fairy lights and hanging bulbs, giving the place a festive atmosphere. And it's busy. I have no doubt Rafe would've thrown plenty of money around to get us the prime table by the window.

I take off my leather jacket and slide into my seat. The hostess appears and says something about getting us drinks. The bell-like tone of her voice makes me look up.

Her hair is strawberry-blond, a warm, golden color with fiery copper highlights.

Her face is angelic. More than that. Exquisite. She's

cute but also gorgeous. She radiates a sweet, dazzling glow that is quite literally lighting up the room.

I realize I'm staring.

She's waiting for me and her expression is intrigued but slightly hassled. They're busy tonight and I'm holding her up. She has other things to do besides stand here and wait for me.

But I take my time. I can't help it. I want to watch her a little more. Check out the soft, bright colors of her. The deep blue shade of her eyes and her long eyelashes that blink at me as she waits. The sprinkling of freckles across her nose reminds me of summer. The mesmerizing pinkness of her lips and her pale, clear skin is fascinating me.

I'm stunned. More than that. I'm slayed.

I want to spend some time just watching her and drinking in every detail.

This is not something that's ever happened to me before.

But I can't pull my eyes away.

She's slim but curvy in all the right places. *Damn. All the right places.* Maybe I've just gone too long without and I'm suddenly suffering the hellish consequences of my self-imposed monk-like existence. My chest feels tight and my heart's pumping fast. She's so fucking *beautiful.* My cock—*fuck*—goes instantly rock hard.

Damn it.

Max. Calm the fuck down.

The combination of her glow and her sweet, hot,

completely-unaware-of-it cuteness quite literally hits me like a ton of bricks.

I won't act on it. Of course I won't. I'm a guy who ruins people's lives. A loose cannon, they call me. A rebel who never toes the line. A guy who uses women and breaks their hearts.

She's way too pure for the likes of me.

I'd dirty her with all my darkness. I'd rain all over her glowing sunny day.

I can't help fantasizing, though, just for a minute. What would it be like? To ask her out? On a real date. I honestly don't know if I've ever been on one.

I try to picture it. A wholesome, glorious, strawberry blond, blue-eyed, spectacularly dazzling date.

Or maybe two.

Or ten.

Ten thousand.

Ten fucking million, all strung together so there's no separation between them.

Fuck.

2

———

I NOTICE him as soon as he steps inside the door. Of course I do. He's too gorgeous *not* to notice. He's tall and muscular but lean and gold-lit, like a renegade gypsy someone dressed up in business clothes and tried to disguise as one of their own.

The restaurant is busy tonight. If it was anyone else, I wouldn't have waited. I would have left the menus and come back once they'd had a chance to decide. But something about him holds my attention—very persuasively. Like he's insisting on it.

"We're out of shrimp," says Sophie, as she glides past with a full tray of plates.

"The asshole at table seven says his steak is too rare," mutters Jessie, precariously balancing four glasses of white wine.

"Someone at the bar wants to order five blueberry pies to go and we only have three left," says Louis, the busboy.

It's one of those insane nights. Two of my waitstaff called in sick and I'm covering four tables as well as hostessing and serving drinks. I'd been baking since five a.m., cooking and organizing orders all day, and working the floor since the dinner service started at six. And I haven't been sleeping well for reasons I don't even want to think about.

But that's what it takes to make it work in this industry. Mostly I love it.

We've only been open for three months and already my business is booming and the orders for pies are pouring in. I never planned for the pies to become such a big part of the business, but once people taste them, they just keep on coming back for more. It's nothing new. I baked my first pie when I was five years old, back home in Georgia. It wasn't long before people started asking for them and placing orders. When I was seven, I charged a dollar a pie. In high school, I charged ten. I cooked for pocket money, then put myself through cooking school. Then, four months ago, I moved to L.A. with what was left of my savings, plus a small loan from Grandma Bea— which, if business continues to be as good as it's been, I'll be able to pay back sooner than I'd planned.

I scouted around and found the perfect location for the restaurant, upmarket enough but two blocks off the main tourist shopping trails so rent is still pretty reasonable. I redecorated it to look exactly like I dreamed it would. And all that hard work is finally paying off. Three months ago I'd hung out my sign—*Peach's*—and never looked back.

Each day is just a little busier than the last. I need to hire more staff. Every one of us is being run off our feet tonight, not that I can complain.

The scene is noisy and the bar is crowded with that perfect L.A. mix of hipsters, fashion types, Hollywood wannabes, tourists and suits. So different to Georgia. It's just before eight p.m. and the crowd is happily buzzed and relaxed after a hard day of working or dreaming of the big time or sightseeing or shopping. I tuck a stray curl behind my ear as I walk up to the new arrivals who'd called ahead to reserve the best table. And offered three hundred dollars for the privilege. Fine by me.

The menu here at Peach's is good, I make sure of that. It's also expensive. They get what they pay for. And so far our reviews have been nothing but glowing.

Despite the noise, the crowd, the demands from both the customers and the kitchen, I can't help but come to a quiet stop after I lead the group of four to their table and wait for them to take their seats.

Their party consists of two men and two women. The two men look like brothers. Brothers that just so happened to have stepped off of a pirate-themed Ralph Lauren shoot. They're *that* ruggedly glamorous, but it's the younger one who holds my attention. He's ridiculously good-looking. It's the kind of over-the-top good looks that stop traffic. But his looks aren't the only thing I notice. His brooding charisma colors everything about him. He has dark hair that curls in loose flicks over his collar. He's wearing a leather jacket. The day's stubble darkens his square jaw, and there are pronounced shadows under his very-blue eyes.

He shrugs off the jacket and his hard-looking and bulked-up muscles—it would be impossible not to notice them—strain under the cotton of his expensive-looking business shirt. His sleeves are rolled up and he's not wearing a tie. He has tattoos on his lower arms and the base of his tanned, corded neck. He slides into his seat.

Wow.

I have a weird urge to just stand there and appreciate him for a while, like he's a work of art or something.

He's probably one of those playboys who thinks he's God's gift to womankind. A subdued, perceptive arrogance is practically radiating off him.

He's staring right at me, watching me with his jungle-cat eyes like he knows how beautiful he is. Like he's challenging me to look away.

I don't.

I *can't*, more accurately.

His alert attention burns into me and I feel the heat of him, weirdly. In my racing heartbeat and in the low pit of my stomach. And lower.

Jesus, Peach. Calm down, girl.

Strangely, though, under his burly, tough-guy looks, there's something else, too. A deep-rooted vulnerability that would be easy to miss. Under all that masculine over-confidence, there's a spark of something much harder to read.

I find myself wondering what it would feel like to touch a strand of his hair, to see if it's as thick as it looks. Or to talk to him in a quiet moment and find out what caused those bruise-like shadows under his eyes. To feed him some of my homemade Georgia pie and gently coax from him a confession about what kind of past could possibly spark that haunted look that fringes somewhere behind the dark light of his eyes.

Of course I'll never find out. He's a paying customer on what appears to be a double date.

The only ring he's wearing is a gold band on his left pinkie. There's a chunky silver cuff around his wrist with illuminated red lights on it.

It looks like one of those home-detention cuffs you see on crime TV.

Jesus H. He's a *criminal!* Probably newly released from jail or something. Definitely one to steer well clear of.

Another one to steer very well clear of.

Even if he *is* drop-dead beautiful in a danger-edged kind of way.

Even if he is staring at me with an expression that makes my stomach do a funny little flip. I'm only human, after all. A thoroughly female human who's witnessing in its purest form that wild, rare phenomenon: sexy, roughed-up alpha male perfection.

No effing way, Peach, my common sense insists. *Serve him politely then get your ass back to work. He's got trouble written all over him.*

So I smile and begin my little intro. I pride myself on handling any unforeseen situation that crops up in my restaurant and I can handle this one. "Hi, and welcome to Peach's. Your waitress will be with you in just a minute with our specials list for this evening. Can I get ya'll started with a drink from the bar?"

The two women are seated further back in the booth, preoccupied, talking, showing each other pictures on their phones. Working in restaurants and bars for the past six years, and now owning one, I've become pretty good at reading people. I guess at a glance that the older brother and the blond girl are together. Something about their body language, even though they aren't touching, communicates an intimate bond. And she's wearing a ring. Not just any ring, but a gigantic Mount Everest of an engagement ring.

The second woman seems to be there as a friend of the blond. Maybe the older brother and his fiancée are trying to set the younger brother up with the other girl.

But Hottie doesn't seem all that interested in her. At all.

I could be wrong, of course. I don't think I am,

though. Partly because he's still staring at me. And he's not just looking at me like he's thinking about what type of beer he wants to order. He's staring at me with a sort of layered fascination that's making me blush even more.

The older brother, thankfully, breaks the trance we seem to be mired in. "We'll have a bottle of Krug. 1998 if you have it. I'll have a Jack Daniel's on ice and…Max?"

So his name is Max.

He's still watching me. He finally says, "What's your name?" The low, husky sound of his voice hits me somewhere just below my navel.

The older brother turns to watch him, like something about his question, or the way he asks it, is slightly out of character.

"Peach," I tell him.

"Peach," he drawls, raising one perfect eyebrow, like he doesn't quite believe me. It's nowhere near a smile, but the barely-playful vibe softens the harder edges of him, which only adds to his beauty.

Damn, is what I'm thinking.

"Isn't this restaurant called Peach's?" That rasp to his deep voice unnerves me a little. There's something borderline irresistible about the sound of it. Low, layered bass notes that make you wonder about things you shouldn't be wondering about.

"It's my restaurant." I make sure I smile, partly so I don't come across as out-of-breath, which is how I almost feel. Almost.

"You're a chef?"

"And a baker, a hostess and sometimes a bartender. I sort of do it all."

"A baker," he repeats. I'm usually pretty good at figuring people out, but this guy's got some serious layers going on. For a second I think I might have mistaken his interest for sarcasm, but when I glance at his brother's face, I can see that he's watching this play out, like there's something going on here that he hasn't witnessed before.

"Best apple pie in the city, according to the Times," comments the brother.

This makes me smile. I appreciate that. My pie is, after all, my pride and joy. I framed the Times review and hung it in a special place at the entrance of the restaurant. It was the kind of review I dreamed about.

"No shit," says Hottie. "Do *you* make the apple pie?"

"Sure do."

"What kind of name is Peach? Is that your real name?" Like he's perfectly entitled to ask me the most personal questions imaginable. Never offend your customers, however, is Rule Number One, so I keep my tone chatty and fun.

"Nope. My real name is Dixie May Rafferty Sutton. But most people have been calling me Peach since I was around five years old. Ever since I baked my first pie, actually. It was a peach pie, in case you're wondering."

"Can't get any more Southern than that," says his brother.

But Hottie—Max—has this mesmerized look on his face. "I *was* wondering, as a matter of fact." Then he says something that makes me go cold. "What happened to your eye?"

I feel that sick, lingering anger—and fear, even though I swore I wouldn't be afraid of the asshole who did this. I'd tried to cover it up with make-up but the bruise must still be visible.

"Oh, that?" I say, as breezily as I can muster, touching my cheek. "I walked into a door. Rushing around as much as I do, it happens." I haven't told a single person about the...*incident,* and I'm sure not about to tell this total stranger.

The brothers glance at each other briefly before looking back up at me. I feel wildly uncomfortable being scrutinized by them like some kind of victim. I was actually hoping the whole situation would just go away by itself. That it was a one-off. The police put a restraining order in place but one of them commented that, unless you have a round-the-clock bodyguard, restraining orders aren't all that effective.

Either way, he hasn't been back since.

And no one's noticed that I've been sleeping in the tiny closet-sized room I use as an office, so I don't have to walk the three blocks back to my apartment alone at night, or even catch a ride. There's a dark courtyard I have to walk through to get to my door, which is where it happened. I'm too terrified to go back there. I'd rather die than flee back to Georgia, even though I've thought about it. A lot. But I've worked too hard for this. And I'm made of stronger stuff than that. At least I hope I am.

I'll figure it out.

I do my best to regain my composure. "So, have you decided what you'd like to order?"

I can't help but notice that Max is still staring at me. But the look on his face has changed. There's no longer any traces of smugness or amusement. He looks angry. Furious, in fact. His fist clenches, which makes the muscles of his arm look even more ripped. *Holy hell.*

And this is just what I don't *need in my life. Another criminal with rage issues.*

Anyway, it's none of his business. I don't know him and he doesn't know me or anything about me. The only thing he needs to know about is how kick-ass my pie is.

And then Max says, "I'll also have a Jack Daniel's on ice. And to start, I want a double slice of apple pie, served warm with vanilla ice cream on the side." The way he looks at me when he says it…it almost sounds like he's ordering *me* as a side dish.

I can feel myself blush, but I've already made my mind up about him. "I *always* serve it warm with vanilla ice cream on the side," I tell him. "*Homemade* vanilla ice cream."

His face, when I mention this, loses all traces of that self-assured tough-guy sneer. For a brief few seconds, he looks kind and sincere and so heartbreakingly beautiful my heart skips a beat.

No way, honey. Get back to work. Right this minute.

Reclaiming my sanity just in time, I smile. My professional, hostess smile. And then I leave them to it and get on with my job.

3

———

"Send me all of it," I tell Mike.

Mike Finch is the one and only person at my company I trust completely. I met him at Stanford, where I did my MBA. Before you go assuming that I'm a genius or some studious academic type, I'll fill you in on the real story. My brother gave some huge-ass endowment to the school to buy my admission. At that point in my life I wasn't exactly Stanford material, not even close, so it took a little coercion and a huge wad of cash to get me anywhere near Palo Alto. They put a new wing on the library, that's the kind of money we're talking. But once I got there I decided to make the most of it. I ended up graduating near the top of my class. Mike graduated right behind me. So when Rafe offered me a job running Downtown Investments a year ago, I talked him into hiring Mike. Mike's so loyal he threatened to quit if they didn't keep me on after the whole insider trading fiasco. I told him to stay put so he could be my eyes and ears in the office.

I need him in place if I'm going to figure out who screwed me over.

"I've got all the security camera footage on file," Mike says, "which I'll email you tonight, once I get home and off the radar. I'm still waiting on the spyware password so we can start looking through all the emails, logins, surfing activity and so on. Your brother's the only one who knows it."

"He's out of town. I'm supposed to talk to him tomorrow."

"Great," he says. "Hey, you want to grab a beer later, Max? I haven't seen you since you've been in lock-down."

"I can't tonight. But I'll give you a call soon. Yeah, we're overdue."

"And I'll keep you posted if I hear anything."

"Thanks, man. I owe you one."

"Max, I owe you about ten. It's the least I can do."

"I appreciate it."

I end the call. I think about calling Rafe tonight but decide not to. It can wait. He went AWOL for a couple days after Lexi left him on what was supposed to be their wedding day, when his crazy bitch of an ex showed up at the altar announcing she was pregnant. Which was a lie but they didn't find that out until I made her get a court-ordered pregnancy test. Long story short: he totally lost his shit and disappeared at sea for three days. I was about to break out of my zone to go and find him. Luckily, the Coast Guard beat me to it. The two of them worked through it and now he and Lexi are married and on their honeymoon in Italy.

I'm not sure I want to interrupt all that. I feel like those two just need some time to themselves.

Home detention's not all bad. I've had an idea for a business that's been rolling around in my head for a while that I'm starting to look into. I spend a few hours each day following my brokers online and advising them by phone. I work out for four hours a day. I sleep. I eat.

It could be worse. It could be a lot fucking worse. I could be in prison. And I've spent enough time in juvie to know that prison is definitely someplace I don't ever want to be.

It's been a long time since I've been alone this much. It's kicking up a few memories of the loneliest time of my life that are definitely best left un-fucking-remembered.

I need to get out of this apartment for a while.

I'm hungry. No, I'm fucking *starving.* I'm so voracious I feel like I could go insane with it. On about a million different levels.

I've been fighting against my urges for more than a week but I can't take it anymore.

My hope was that she would fade out of my mind. That I'd just sort of forget about her.

That hasn't happened.

At first I wouldn't allow myself to think about her. I'd go to the gym and force myself into a state of physical exertion so intense my mind would go blank. After a few days of this, entrancing images of her started to leech in my brain, no matter how hard I tried to hold them back.

That outrageously sweet body, in her tight little black outfit.

That seraphic face, like a goddamn angel's. I've honestly never seen such a beautiful face in my entire life.

Those perfect, pink lips and that sweet-as-honey Southern accent.

My real name's Dixie May Rafferty Sutton. Of course it is. *It was a peach pie, in case you're wondering.*

I could go down there and have a slice of that warm apple pie and homemade ice cream that's so good it'll blow your goddamn head off.

Problem is, I know if I go, I'll never leave.

I'll need more.

I'll need everything.

And I don't want to do that to her.

I'm a fuck-up, no doubt about it. A certified, grade-A piece of damaged goods. I don't want to inflict my darkness on all that cute Southern gorgeousness for my own twisted pleasure. I don't want to bring her down, with all my baggage and my history, like a black cloud storming all over her perfect world.

It's taken every ounce of willpower I possess to stay away.

I peel off my sweat-soaked clothes and step into the shower. I let the scalding water run down my body. I just finished yet another ridiculously-intense workout and my muscles are wound tight. The water feels good.

That body.

No.

Those candy-pink lips.

Max, leave her alone.

Those eyes. Watching me, all deep-blue and perceptive. Almost like she was seeing more of me than just my looks and my money.

I imagine what she would *feel* like. I imagine the smoothness of that flawless skin. How soft she'd be. I imagine what she would *taste* like. Sugar and sunshine and peach pie.

I'd start by slowly peeling off her clothes, licking every inch of her skin. I'd make her squirm. I'd tease her. I'd suck on her taut, pink nipples until she moaned and begged me to take her. Fuck, she'd be so sweet.

My cock is hard as a fucking rock, pulsing with hot agony.

I feel dizzy with lust and need and rage.

Because I can't do it.

I can't stay away.

I've kept myself away for eleven days, twenty-two hours and forty-seven minutes and I can't take another second of it.

I place my hand against the Italian tiles and curse myself.

Max, you fucking lunatic. Leave. Her. The. Fuck. Alone.

But I'm too far gone. I just want to *see* her, I tell myself. I don't have to do anything more than order a slice of pie. Just to be near her for a few minutes and bask in her strawberry-blond glow.

I like to think I might have had the will-power to stay away, to save her from myself, if it weren't for one detail.

That faint hint of a bruise around her eye. It didn't look like the kind of bruise you'd get if you walked into a door, I know that much. I also know what it means when you flinch when someone asks you how it happened. *Because I know what it feels like to flinch like that, and to hide the truth.*

She denied it. Maybe she *did* run into a door. Maybe she didn't. It's that ambiguity that makes my decision.

It's possible that someone hurt her.

Maybe she needs me.

Don't be delusional, you asshole. You're no knight in shining armor. You're a deviant. A criminal. A black sheep. Leave her the fuck alone.

But I already know that's one thing I can't do. Until I know for sure.

If there's the slightest chance that that little angel needs help, then I'm going to fucking help her.

You're the very last thing she needs.

Maybe I'm the very thing she *does* need.

Get over yourself, Max. You're a twisted fuck-up without a conscience.

This happens to me every now and then. The voices in my head try to talk me into stuff or out of it. This time, I ignore them. My path is glaringly clear. The fire in me is fierce. *Crazy*-fierce.

I need to see her again.

To make sure she's okay, that's all.

I pull on some jeans, a shirt and my leather jacket.

I take the elevator down and step out onto the street. There's a vendor on the corner selling bunches of pink roses. I've never bought flowers before in my life but I do it now. I buy two bunches and the guy wraps them into a huge bouquet.

All the women I pass are staring at me.

It's late. Before I can think too much or talk myself out of it, I start walking toward Peach's.

4

MY MOTHER MET the love of her life when she was seventeen years old. He was twenty and Irish, traveling the world with nothing but his backpack, his brogue and twinkling blue eyes that could have charmed the pants off a nun, according to her. She should know, too. Her parents sent her to a strict Southern school that also served as a convent. My parents fell madly in love at first sight and married three months later. By the time they took their vows, I was already on the way. My grandfather didn't approve of the marriage and disowned my mother from his vast fortune, made over several generations with his family's four hundred acres of peach tree orchards. As it turned out, my mother would have lost her inheritance anyway since my grandfather had a gambling problem no one knew about until it was too late.

My parents were living in a shack when I was born,

blissfully happy with hardly a dime to their names. My father worked as a field hand. My one and only memory of him, when I was four years old, was in the late afternoon summer sun as he walked up the driveway to our tiny house, his hands dirty, his skin tanned, his eyes such a deep shade of blue they looked like stolen jewels, his red hair wild and gleaming, the color of polished copper. When he saw us, sitting on the porch swing waiting for him, his face broke into the happiest smile I've ever seen, before or since.

Two days later he was killed when a truck hit him as he was walking along the side of the road.

My mother was inconsolable for two years. She cried so hard and so much her tears ran dry, she said. Then, stubborn Southern belle that she was, she picked herself up and dusted herself off and went in search of husband number two. Knowing she'd never find true love again, this time she went after a man with money. He took her skiing in the Swiss Alps on their honeymoon, where she skied right off a cliff on a triple black diamond trail. She'd never skied before in her life, so what she was doing on a triple black diamond trail in the first place was anyone's guess. I know what *my* guess is.

I like to think she knew I was in good hands. After I became an orphan, I went to live with my Grandma Bea, my mother's mother, who suspected her husband's gambling habit early on and had quietly put away a not-so-modest savings for herself. She used her savings to hire a fancy divorce lawyer from Atlanta who won her the grand old plantation house but zero money to maintain it. We didn't care. We tended the rose garden and picked the peaches. We baked peach pies, apple pies, blueberry pies, cherry pies. We baked bread and cookies and brownies and made homemade ice cream. We cooked French recipes with butter and wine and tomatoes we grew ourselves. You name it, we baked it and cooked it and served it to her three best friends who practically lived with us—which was hardly surprising since we fed them so well.

Grandma Bea said I had a knack. "You were born for this, darlin'," she said.

I knew she was right. The powdery flour on my fingers and the sweet peaches baked into those sugary pies made me happy. In the kitchen, I was in my element.

I always planned on opening my own restaurant. I decided it would be better to open a restaurant in a big city than in our tiny town in Georgia. I could make my own money. Maybe even *lots* of money. I could pay Grandma Bea back and fix up her house so she wouldn't have to worry anymore.

I also felt that spark of wanderlust I must have inherited from my father. I'll end up back in Georgia one day, when the time is right, but first I need to see the world. Or at least some of it.

So, five months ago, I packed up my suitcase, hugged Grandma Bea and took a Greyhound bus west.

Turns out I feel closer to my daddy—not that I ever really knew him—when I'm on the road. Four days on a Greyhound bus is a lot of time to think. I wondered about the love my parents had. I wondered if I'd ever find anything half as real as that. More than likely, I won't. One, I'm too busy building my business. Two, I avoid dating, even though I got asked out by pretty much every boy in my town. Grandma Bea and her friends used to tease me about it. But look what happened to my parents. Their love ended up killing my mother because she couldn't bear to live without it. I watched her cry herself to sleep for two whole years. I was at an impressionable age and it sunk in. I'm just not sure all that pain is worth it.

When I got to L.A., I found a tiny apartment with a small courtyard.

And, after decorating exactly as I'd always planned, the restaurant launch was more than I'd ever dreamed. The very first week I got some big-name influencers raving about my pies and my menu. We've been packed and run off our feet ever since.

But then, like a cloud moving over the sun, things started to change. All because of a random customer who came in one afternoon, just after the lunch rush was over. He had short, almost crew-cut light brown hair. He was stocky. And strong-looking in a way that put me on edge even though I wasn't sure why. Everything about him was sort of nondescript. Almost like he was deliberately *trying* to be difficult to describe. There was something unusually quiet and withdrawn about him. But alert. He was watching everyone, as though measuring our movements and our schedules. I later learned he wasn't watching *us*.

He was watching me.

He sat in the corner reading the newspaper, drinking cup after cup of coffee until the staff started commenting. Sophie served him, but he'd requested me. Since The Customer Is Always Right and so on, I'd taken his table. He already knew my name was Peach, which I guess is obvious enough. He asked me out for a drink after my shift. I turned him down, telling him I was too busy. I wished him a good afternoon, hoping he would leave, which he eventually did and that was that.

Except that wasn't that.

He started coming in every afternoon. Each day, he asked me out. Each day, I politely refused. After four straight days of this, I saved my paperwork so I could retreat into my office and not have to feel the eerie awareness of being watched.

After that, I stopped walking back to my apartment. After I closed up the restaurant at night, I'd get a ride instead. But by then, it was too late. Somewhere along the line, he'd followed me.

He knew where I lived.

It happened fifteen days ago, to be precise—when something like that happens, the details etch themselves into your memory, deeply, where you don't expect them to.

It was just past midnight. I was walking through my little courtyard, ready to collapse into bed from a long day that had started at 5 a.m.

Seeing the stranger step out from behind a concrete column near the door of my apartment was the single most terrifying moment of my life.

Why won't you go out with me, he'd said, as though our meeting was a casual coincidence.

I was too scared to be polite. I said something rude. More rude than I usually would.

He'd stepped forward and slapped me across the face, with his hand closed. Hard. So hard I saw stars.

In her day, my Grandma Bea had been a real looker, according to those who knew her. She was also a tomboy with three older brothers and she taught me how to knee a man where it hurts the most when times call for such a thing.

That night was one of those times. My stalker fell to the ground, giving me enough time to get into my apartment, lock the door and call the police. But by the time they got there, he was long gone. That's when I learned that a restraining order isn't always effective. Unless you've got a full-time bodyguard, the police can't be on hand to enforce it every second of the night and day. They do the best they can, they assured me.

Which didn't assure me at all.

What if I hadn't fought back? What if my knee-jerk reaction hadn't stopped him? What would he have done?

These questions plague me. I haven't been back to my apartment since. I use the gym across the street to shower and that's the only place I go, with Sophie. I've been working late and bunking down in my tiny office.

The stranger hasn't been back but I don't for a second think he won't come back. The whole thing terrifies me in a way that's taking its toll, I can admit. I like to think of myself as staunch, like my Grandma Bea who's as tough as they come, but some days it's tiring to pretend I'm not scared.

What if he does it again? What if he's mad now? What if he hurts me? Or worse? What if he kills me?

I've tried to put it out of my mind. But it won't go away. I haven't been sleeping well and after two weeks of this, I'm exhausted.

I gave notice on my apartment. I can't even bring myself to go back there to pick up my stuff, not that there's much of it. The landlord said there's a new tenant that wants to move in next Saturday. So I called a moving company to pack up the few boxes that had never been fully unpacked in the first place, and asked them to deliver them here.

This isn't like me at all. I don't *give up*. I power on through. But I don't want to live my life watching over my shoulder. Being attacked like that shook me up. Badly. For the first time in my life, I don't know what to do.

"You want a drink, Peach?" asks Johnny, the bartender, and I jump a little. God. I need to get a grip. Johnny notices my reaction.

The service has ended and I'm sitting at the bar, going through the night's receipts on my iPad as Johnny puts the clean wine glasses back into their hanging racks. "Sure, why not. Let's have a round."

"This Sauvignon Blanc from New Zealand's a good one." He sets three glasses on the bar and pours the wine.

"Thanks, Johnny." I take a sip. It's cold and tastes good.

"Everything okay, Peach?" Since I hired him three months ago, Johnny and I have become good friends and he's told me some of his backstory, since we usually have a drink together at the end of the night, like tonight, when I'm going through the receipts and he's cleaning up the bar after we've closed up. He's tall and slim and hand-some, with dark blond hair and green eyes. He moved here from Minneapolis six months ago and is about as flamboyantly gay as a person can be.

"Charlie is meeting me here. Oh, there he is." Johnny goes over to the door and lets in his new crush, who I've met once before.

"Hi, Charlie."

"Hey, Peach." Charlie kisses me on both cheeks then does the same to Johnny, and sits next to me at the bar. Johnny serves him a glass of wine.

Charlie's very good-looking, with black hair and a

killer suit. He's some kind of computer whiz and runs his own business that has something to do with Internet security or something along those lines. Johnny described it to me once and it sounds very high-tech. Johnny also told me Charlie almost got arrested when he was fourteen for hacking in to the FBI's website.

"I was just telling Peach she needs to take a break from this place," Johnny tells Charlie. "She works too much."

I've been trying to keep it inconspicuous to the staff that I've been sleeping in my office. I covered up my bruise with make-up and it seems to have worked. No one asked about it. Now I'm wondering if they suspect that something's going on.

I try to change the subject. "How's business going, Charlie?"

"Gangbusters. I'm getting run off my feet. But I can basically charge whatever I want, so there's that."

"You should see Charlie's apartment," says Johnny. "It's to die for. And don't change the subject, sweetie. You really do need a break."

Sophie joins us, overhearing. "Let's go dancing! We could hit that club that's right down the road. Peach needs some fun and so do I."

Fun.

Sophie's got dark hair and dark eyes and is one of those rare people who's actually *from* L.A., born and raised.

Sure I could. I should. It'll be fine. I'll be with friends. Besides, I *do* feel like a night out. I haven't done enough exploring in my new city. I'm definitely not finding the sweet spot between that work and life balance yet, but I guess that's to be expected when you're just starting out.

I suddenly get a pang of homesickness for the peach orchards and the rose garden. And my grandmother and her laughing friends. The feeling of *safety*.

But I can stay strong, for Grandma Bea. If I'm going to pay for the refurbishments to her house and restore it to its former glory, I *have* to stay strong. So she can live out her retirement in style, like she deserves.

"Let's go out and see if we can find ourselves some hot and available hunks," says Sophie, clinking her glass against mine, then Johnny's.

Right.

A random memory comes to me, of a customer who came in around a week or so ago. The outrageously beautiful one, with the criminal's bracelet and the dark blue eyes. Max, his brother had called him.

I wonder how he liked his pie.

He hasn't been back.

It makes me feel sad, weirdly, that the *other* random stranger came back, but not that one.

Life really does have a sick sense of humor.

He was clearly another Mr. Wrong, but there'd been something so…magnetic about him.

Or he was just crazily hot, Peach, and jolted you out of the nun-like state of nothingness you reside in.

That's to protect my heart, I remind myself. So I don't end up like my poor mother, skiing off a cliff because she couldn't live without her one true love.

Occasionally—like now—it occurs to me that I shouldn't let my mother's sorrow hold me back. I'm twenty-one years old and have never in my life been on a real date. Avoidance makes things easy. But it also makes them sort of…dull. Maybe Sophie is right. If I wasn't so scared of being stalked, I might actually let loose and have some fun.

We lock up for the night and we walk down the street. I keep an eye out but there's no sign of anyone following us.

The club is only three blocks away, and when we get inside, it's crowded and dimly lit with strobe lights and fake smoke and a red glow from the corner where the DJ is set up. The dance floor is throbbing with people, who are either high on life or something more.

So *this* is what normal people do.

We find a booth to sit in and we order a round of drinks. After the glass of wine earlier and two rum and cokes I start to feel a little bit tipsy. Sophie drags me onto the dance floor and we dance for a while in the seething, sweaty crowd. I'm mainly dancing with Sophie but there are a couple of guys who join us. The music's loud and the dance floor is packed. One of the guys starts bumping into me and I can't tell if he's doing it on purpose or if he's just drunk. I'm starting to feel woozy.

"I'm just going to go find the bathroom," I tell Sophie. I need a break for a second. "I'll be right back."

She waves and turns back to the guy she's dancing with. I make my way off the dance floor and deeper into the back of the club.

That's when I see him.

It's him.

It's the freaking stalker.

He has his hood pulled up, covering his hair. But he's wearing the same faded jean jacket he wore the night he waited for me outside my apartment. He's leaning against a back wall, alone. Watching the crowd.

The panic crackles in my brain like an electric current. My heart jolts, my heartbeat racing. *Has he seen me?*

No. He's not looking in my direction.

I duck down.

I have to get out of here. Now.

I make my way through the tightly-packed crowd. I'm pushing my way through, but it's too slow. Finally, I get to the entrance. I slip out the front door.

Terror has a taste. It's bitter in my mouth, like blood. I look behind me. It's only a few blocks to the restaurant. If I can…*oh shit.*

No.

No.

It's him.

He's pushing his way out the door. *He sees me.*

He's coming after me.

I run for my life.

Jesus Christ! Is this really happening?

I could scream. I could grab someone and beg for help. There are a few people around. Would they help me? Would it make a difference? Would they be able to save me?

I can't risk it. I keep running.

I turn the corner, onto the street where my restaurant is, and I crash into something hard, which stops me in my tracks.

It's not a something, it's a some*one*.

It takes me a few seconds to comprehend that there are pink flower petals everywhere and the scent of roses almost overwhelms me.

Someone's blocking my way. Someone big and rock-hard and…holding a large and now very decimated bunch of flowers.

Holy hell.

It's him.

It's that beautiful…*Max* with the muscles and the blue eyes who came to the restaurant and ordered apple pie for dinner and whose party left an enormous tip.

The only thing I can think to say to him is, "Please help me."

I look behind me and see the stalker turning the

corner. He doesn't look as big as he did before. Not compared to Max, who's—now that I'm standing behind him like he's a shield—*huge*. Strong and tough and muscular as hell. And *mean*-looking. In a good way. In exactly the kind of way I need him to be right now.

Max seems to immediately read what's going on here. "Do you want me to kill him?" he says to me in a low voice.

"No. I want you to help me get away from him. Please."

Max is a wall of solid, furious muscle.

The stalker stops walking as soon as he sees Max. Max's voice is deep and menacing when he says, "If I ever see you again or if you ever so much as come within a goddamn mile of this girl I will personally make it my life's mission to hunt you down and kill you so slowly and so painfully you'll be begging me to fucking hurry it up. Do you understand me?"

The stalker doesn't reply. He turns and disappears around the corner.

For now, at least, he's gone.

Holy fuck.

I look up at Max. He's blurry and I realize there are tears of relief in my eyes.

He's big and panther-dark but there's not a thing about him that feels threatening to me. "Are you all right?" he says.

"I...I think so."

"Come on. Let's get you somewhere safe."

"If you could just walk me to the restaurant—" My voice sounds strange. Terrified, which isn't surprising.

His expression is dark. He walks with me up the street toward the restaurant, looking back once to see if anyone is following us. I follow his gaze but the street is empty.

We get to the restaurant and I unlock the door. He comes in with me. I don't ask him to leave. I'm not ready to be alone.

"I'm going to call the cops and report this, while he's still in the area," Max says. "All right?"

It's nice of him to offer it. "Okay." Even though he's still wearing his criminal's bracelet. I find myself hoping he doesn't get into trouble for this. By somehow being involved.

Max makes the phone call. A couple of officers arrive and ask a lot of questions and I tell them everything. I tell them about the earlier incident outside my apartment and in some ways I'm glad Max overhears everything. So I don't have to explain it again. And because there's something so damn comforting about his presence. He's a total stranger, but there's a depth to him that feels calm. And compassionate. Like he's absorbing my confession, and—weirdly—taking some of the burden as his own.

One of the officers gives me a watch-like bracelet with a call button on it, strapping it onto my wrist. "This will track your whereabouts and if you run into the attacker again, push the button and we'll be with you in approximately five minutes."

I thank the guy, but…five minutes? A lot of damage can be done in five minutes.

Max is sitting at the bar. They ask him a few more questions, then they leave.

"Nice bling," he says.

"We match." It's ironic, I guess. His and hers tracking cuffs. "Thank you, Max."

"You remember my name. Oh. Right. I told the police."

"I remembered you. From the other night. You were kind of memorable."

"So were you." It's impossible not to notice how absurdly good-looking he is. He's not just beautiful and beefed-up and masculine as hell, he's also perceptive in a way that makes you feel like you'll be safe with him, even though his sheer size and obvious strength should be intimidating.

"Would you like a drink?" I ask him. "I owe you one."

"I'll have one if you have one."

Whatever buzz I had earlier in the evening is completely gone. Nothing like sheer terror to sober you up. "What'll you have?"

"Jack Daniels on ice would be great."

I pour two and slide Max his drink. My phone rings and I take it out of my pocket. It's Sophie. "Hey," I answer.

I can hear the thump of the music in the background. "Where'd you go?" she yells.

"Sorry to disappear like that. I…ran into someone. A friend," I bluff. "I'm back at the restaurant. I was just about to call you."

"Are you okay?"

"Yeah, fine. Tired. You guys have a good night, though, okay? I'll see you tomorrow."

"I can't believe you bailed before we found you a hot and available hunk!" she laughs.

"I'll leave that up to you. Have fun, Soph."

I don't bother telling her about the hunk I'm currently having a drink with. Or that he might possibly be the hunkiest hunk of any hunk on planet Earth. But of course it's not like that. It was just a chance meeting— and thank God for that. He was exactly *where* I needed him *when* I needed him. A knight in a shining leather jacket with tattoos and a criminal's cuff and a huge bouquet of roses.

"I'm sorry about your flowers." Obviously a gift for someone. Someone who's probably waiting for him right now, wondering where he is. "I don't want to keep you from wherever you were going. Thank you again for…" I stop before I say *saving me*. It sounds too intense, even if it's true.

"You haven't told anyone what happened to you the other night?" He takes a sip of his drink. He doesn't seem to be in a hurry to get to wherever he's going.

"No."

"Why not?"

I don't know why I didn't tell Sophie or Johnny or any of my staff who have become my friends. "They would have worried. I didn't think they needed to do that. It wouldn't have helped."

He considers this. "I'll give you a lift home after we finish these."

"I…" I almost don't say it but, hell, he already knows more about me than anyone else in L.A. It'll hardly make a difference. "I sleep here. I haven't been back to my apartment since it happened. I'm having my stuff moved out."

He's contemplating me. "I can understand why you wouldn't feel safe there."

I don't know what I was expecting from him, but it wasn't this. This interest. This understanding. I remember the first time I saw him. My first impression was that…he was ridiculously hot. My second thought was that he had layers. Interesting layers that clearly included vulnerability on some level, and hidden emotional scars. They'd been as easy to see as the beauty.

Our eyes meet. There's nothing rushed about him. He's taking his time.

"The cops said they'd be patrolling the area," I say. "Don't feel like you need to stay. Thanks for everything. Really. But I'll be okay." I feel a light sting behind my eyes as the words almost stick in my throat. I guess I'm still shaken, even if I'm trying not to be. *Am* I okay?

Max glances around the restaurant. "Where do you sleep?"

"There's a reclining chair in my office."

His phone, which is still sitting on the bar, pings with an incoming message. *Bella,* flashes up on the screen. He glances at it but doesn't pick it up.

"Who were the flowers for?" I regret it as soon as I ask the question. Of course it's none of my business.

"You." He tips back the last of his drink.

I stare at him, lightly biting my lip. He must be joking.

"I know what this is going to sound like," he says, "but I'm going to say it anyway. First of all, you've probably noticed this." He glances at his metal cuff. "I was framed for insider trading. I didn't do it. Just so you know. Second, my apartment is literally right around the corner. There are two guest bedrooms with king-sized beds and nice views and their own bathrooms. I've got a stocked fridge and more than enough high-tech security to make sure you won't have to worry about anything or anyone."

I'm not sure what he means. "That's…"

"Come with me. At least you can get a good night's sleep that way."

He's offering…? "Max, I'm not going to—"

"I was coming down here to get some pie, and also because I wanted to see you again. I've been thinking about you ever since I came in the other night and I've tried to stay away but I can't. I bought you flowers. When I got here the restaurant was closed. So I was walking back home when I ran into you. Or, when you ran into me."

"Those were…"

"For you. Yes."

"But…why?"

He frowns a little. "*Why* did I buy you flowers?"

Yes. That's exactly what I'm asking.

"It might have been the pie." He smiles sort of mischievously and glances up at me from under the fall of his thick hair, and—*holy hell*. My stomach does a little flip—only because he's the most physically stunning human being I've ever met and it's sort of daunting and endearing and electrifying all at once.

"Would…? I mean…" *Calm down, Peach. Take a deep breath.* I do. "Do you want some pie?"

Max smiles again. "Now that's an offer I can't refuse. But I'm going to have to insist we take it back to my place."

He seems to think I'm coming home with him. Which is crazy. "I can give you one to take with you."

"I'm not leaving unless you come with me," he says calmly, pouring us each another finger of Jack Daniels from the bottle still sitting on the bar.

"I'm fine here. You don't have to—"

"You're not 'fine' here, Peach. You're scared, for good

reason. You're exhausted and strung out. You need a good night's sleep and someone to watch over you so you don't feel afraid."

Did he really just say that?

"I'm going to take you to my apartment. It's safe there. I promise you can trust me."

I have no reason to trust him. Except that there's a darkly honest glint in his eyes that's real and almost play-fully challenging me to refuse him.

"Text your friend my address," he says. "So she knows where you are. My name is Maximillian Black and I'm a partner at the Downtown Investment Group. CFO, no less. Are you impressed yet? Or at least I *was* CFO. Full disclosure: that was before the conviction. But once I prove my innocence that'll all be overturned." He's writing his address down on a cocktail napkin. "If my brother and sister-in-law were in town, I'd get them to vouch for me. They're on their honeymoon, but they're due back in a couple of days."

"They were the ones you had dinner with the other night."

"Yes. They're a little intense right now, so it's probably good they're not around. But if you want me to call them so they can confirm I'm not a psycho killer, I don't mind interrupting them."

He would do that? "No, it's…fine." Am I really considering staying with him?

Max smiles at me again and I can feel myself caving.

Turns out hotness and kindness are one hell of a potent mixture. The thing is, I *am* exhausted and strung out. I'm tired of being strong and pretending I can handle building a business from the ground up while meanwhile being stalked by a twisted freak who's still on the loose.

"Maximillian," I repeat.

"Yeah. Maximillian Apollo Black. My mother had a flair for the dramatic, apparently."

"I like it. It's got a definite ring to it."

I take two pies out of the fridge behind the bar, where we keep the to-go selection. "Here are your pies, Maximillian Apollo Black. An apple and a peach."

"Thank you, Dixie May Rafferty Sutton."

He remembers my name. My real name, that I told him once, more than a week ago. The only person that calls me Dixie May is my Grandma Bea, and only when she's feeling nostalgic about my mother and her beautiful doomed lost love. The sound of it, spoken like that in his deep, careful voice, just about makes me want to tell him all about my hopes and dreams, weirdly. "Should I get some of the homemade ice cream, too?"

"Hell, yeah. So you'll come with me?"

It's his hopefulness that seals the deal. He really is sort of dazzlingly good-looking. The soft, manly earnestness is basically icing on the cake at this point. "A king-sized bed sounds a little too good to pass up."

He takes the pies and his warm hands brush against

mine, which almost makes me second-guess this whole thing. But then he says, "It's okay," with a certainty that makes me want to cry. "You're okay now. I'll make sure of it."

5

———

I'm bad to the bone and irrevocably damaged. I'm twenty-four years old and I've never had anything resembling a real relationship in my life. My all-time record is a two-night stand. I don't believe in true love or love at first sight or any kind of love at all.

Which is why whatever's going on here is hitting me like a goddamn runaway freight train.

My brother's recent obsession made me wonder, sure, if such a thing could ever happen to me. I seriously doubted I was capable of it. Of caring. Of giving a fuck. Of *feeling*.

Turns out I am.

I'm not going to say this is love at first sight. I don't know what the fuck it is. All I know is that something in me has shifted. She needs me. She doesn't even *want* to need me, aside from the protection I can provide. I had to talk her into coming with me.

I can't remember a woman ever not wanting something from me.

They say it happens when you least expect it. I'm not going to try to define whatever's going on here, after two chance meetings that have amounted to approximately ten minutes in her company. But—*fucking hell*—something about this girl has wound itself around me. Tight.

I'm trying not to stare.

The city lights of the night play across her pale face and the gold-copper waves of her hair as I let her in to my apartment building.

She looks around the foyer, which is made almost entirely of white marble. She's nervous. Not scared, but unsure. She's second guessing coming with me.

I don't want her second guessing a goddamn thing, for reasons I'm not entirely sure of. "I have a hot tub," I say. *Why the fuck did I say that? What am I trying to do, impress her? With a goddamn hot tub?*

She smiles lightly. The elevator doors open and she hesitates before following me inside.

It only gets worse, but I keep talking, because I don't want her to feel like the silence is awkward, or give her any reason to change her mind. "There's a gym on the fifth floor. And a yoga studio, if you're into that kind of thing. I have a pool on my balcony, if you like swimming."

"I…" She doesn't finish.

I know what she was going to say. She doesn't have a swimsuit. She's not staying long enough to swim or sit in the hot tub.

She'll sleep in the king-sized bed I've promised her, then in the morning she'll come to her senses after being so spooked she agreed to stay in the apartment of a total stranger. Tonight, she sees me as a savior. Tomorrow, she'll see me as a guy who convinced her against her better judgment to put her up for a night.

I have exactly seven hours to convince her that she needs to stay longer.

The thoughts going through my head are hard to process, only because no thoughts like this have ever entered my brain before. *Stay as long as you want. More than one night. A week. Longer. Move in.*

WTF?

Her eyes are periwinkle blue. It used to be my favorite color in the crayon box, which is a strange thing to remember. But that's the exact color of her eyes. I want to gaze into them. I want to be worthy of her. I don't want my damaged matrix to dirty her glory.

I'll never allow that to happen, I've already decided.

I'll never hurt this girl.

I try to summon everything good about myself. Since before I can even remember, I've been fighting my own demons. They haunt me like sticky shadows that never go away, no matter how sunny the day might be. This girl is all about the light. Even in the state she's in, her presence and her eyes and her hair are so mind-blowingly illuminating and the glow of her is so real, my demons temporarily retreat. I'm broken but I'm not *bad*. Being with her reminds me of that, and the simplicity of how *good* she makes me feel is as sweet as a drug. My first taste. Mainlined straight to my heart.

I know what that sounds like.

Hell. It *feels* even worse than it sounds. It feels potent and somehow…charmed, like she's digitally enhanced or something, surrounded by this radiant aura of good vibes.

Fuck. Listen to me. I sound like a walking cliché. On steroids.

She's watching me watch her.

I'm determined to tread more carefully than I ever have. I need to make sure she doesn't fear me, at all. My urge to protect her at all costs feels more important right now than anything else about me.

She's so damn *beautiful*. Not just her hair, which might have been spun from the purest gold on earth. Or her mouth, the color of perfection. It goes deeper. It shines out of her eyes, a ridiculously appealing cocktail of decency, kindness, courage and light.

She's calmer now, but her lingering fear crackles into me. I feel like my heart is being ripped out of my chest. *Because I know what that feels like.* And seeing it all play out there on her angel's face is just so fucking wrong.

"Peach." I keep my voice gentle. "I know you've been

through something terrifying, but you're okay now. This apartment building is basically Fort Knox. You're safe here. If you want to call your friends and have them come too, you can."

She doesn't immediately speak. After a few seconds she quietly says, "Thank you, Max. For doing this. I just want to sleep for a while, and then I'll be on my way."

"You can sleep as long as you want." Being this close to her has all my senses hyper-aware. The dizzying scent of her is like some sublime mixture of flowers and sweet, sweet honey. My cock hardens fully, pulsing in red-hot throbs of lust, but this only pisses me off. I'm glad for the pies, which I'm holding in their boxes. I keep them strategically placed. But right now I'm more interested in listening to the sound of her voice. And reassuring her. I notice the curl of her eyelashes. The dewy flawlessness of her skin. It seems strange to me that all these little details in themselves could each be so ludicrously perfect. And when you put them all together into one little strawberry-blond package, it's fucking mind-blowing. I could stare at her all night.

I've always been the quiet type, the kind of guy who avoids small talk at all costs. Usually my conversations with women begin and end with me giving gruff demands or one-word answers.

Not tonight.

I find myself chatting away like an idiot. I want to make her smile. I wonder what her laughter sounds like.

"You know, I never got a chance to say it since you didn't come back to our table that night and I couldn't find you when we left. But I consider myself somewhat of an apple pie expert, since it just so happens to be my favorite food. It's what I eat for breakfast."

"It is?"

"Yeah."

"Me too. Every day."

"You do?" All right, fuck. I might have already fallen for this girl from the first moment I saw her—which is kind of pissing me off, because who does that? Even worse, I might have just found my soulmate. No one else I've ever met eats pie for breakfast.

Slow down, champ. Slow waaaaay the fuck down.

"Yes." Her blue eyes light up just a little at this revelation. "Well, I grew up in a peach orchard. We had to do something with all those peaches. Plus we have forty acres of apple trees, too."

She's practically offering, so I ask it. "Where's that?"

"Georgia."

I smile at her, and I almost laugh because...I don't know the fuck why. I just feel like it. I might almost be... *happy.* "We have something in common, then. What I was going to say, by the way, is that your pie is by far the best I've ever tasted."

This is not something to be taken lightly, obviously. "Really?"

"No contest," I assure her, because it's the fucking truth.

She smiles back at me, basically lighting up my world. "Coming from such an expert, that's high praise."

"I'm not just saying that, either. There's not even a close second."

She actually blushes and something inside my mess of a psyche melts a little.

I want to ask her more about where she comes from and who she is. I don't. She's had a hell of a night and it's definitely not the time to pry. I need to take this slow and get it right. If I fuck this up, I might go mad.

So I search for the best of myself, for the heart of gold my brother always talks about that's buried somewhere deep inside all this dark torment. The elevator opens.

She looks up at me. "This is your apartment?"

"Yeah."

She's looking around, like she's amazed by everything. "I can already tell this is the nicest place I've ever stayed."

"I hope it's okay." I'm suddenly very glad I've worked like a maniac for years on end. Now that I have something to show for it, the only person I actually *do* want to show it to is little Peachie Dixie May. I've never had a woman in this apartment before, believe it or not. I don't bring them here. I made that mistake once, years ago, and couldn't get her to leave even though I couldn't actually remember her name.

This time, it's different.

For reasons I can't explain, this time, everything's different.

She almost smiles, like she can't help the sunny side of herself from shining through, despite what she's just been through. My urge to take care of her is burning in me, and it's a strange feeling. So totally new.

I lead her into my apartment, which is nice and so it should be. I paid six million fucking bucks for it.

She stands there for a few seconds just looking around. "Wow," she says. "This place is amazing."

"I bought it the day after my brother hired me."

Peach blinks as she takes in the space and I'm mesmerized again by the sweep of her eyelashes and the deep-blue color of her eyes. "You said you were framed?" She blushes again after she says it, like she's wishing she hadn't asked about that.

I'll tell her anything she wants to know. "Yes. I'm looking into it."

"That's awful."

"We'll nail whoever it was. In the meantime, it's been nice to have some time away from the office. All I've done for the past five years is work."

"I can relate."

"I'm glad you're here," I tell her. I don't mention the part about how I've spent every second since I met her fantasizing about slowly and thoroughly breaking my vow of celibacy all over her, letting the flood gates of my raging desire go wild.

I walk toward the kitchen. The apartment is a huge loft-type space, ultra-modern, open-plan, with two whole walls of windows. One of these walls is folding glass doors leading out to the balcony that my housekeeper leaves open most of the time. They're open now and the pool and hot tub area are surrounded by tropical plants that are lit with small spotlights. "Take a seat on the couch if you want," I tell her. "We'll have some pie and a glass of…what would go with apple pie? Champagne? I think I have some here in the fridge."

She takes a seat on the couch. I heat up the pie and pour the champagne. By the time I walk over to serve them to her, she's fast asleep.

I watch her for a while, trying not to be weird or over-the-top about it. In her sleep, she looks impossibly young. The small spark of my addiction, now that I'm near her, has bloomed into some crazy wildfire rush.

Holy fuck.

I don't know where all this white knight compulsion is coming from, but I'm feeling it. Right down to my heart, where something hot and dazzling is forging there.

You don't have to be afraid anymore, I want to say. *I'll take care of you. You're safe with me.*

Please let that be true.

6

I OPEN MY EYES.

It's so dark in here. I'm in a huge bed.

Who's bed?

It all comes flooding back to me. I'm in that hot gypsy-pirate's apartment. Max Black. *Maximillian Apollo Black,* to be exact.

The stalker followed me. And Max saved me. He rescued me, using his body as a shield.

And then he brought me back here to his ultra-swish apartment. I've never seen anything like this place in my life.

I don't even remember going to bed.

God, I must have fallen asleep on the couch. He must have carried me in here and tucked me in.

It's...sweet. And more than a little mortifying. To crash out right in front of him like that.

I reach into my pocket for my phone. It's not there. I panic for a second, feeling around the bed. Did I lose it?

My eyes adjust to the darkness enough to see that my phone is sitting on the table next to the bed. Along with a glass of water. I'm insanely thirsty. I drink the whole glass.

My phone is dead.

What time is it? Holy shit, I'm probably late for work.

I notice then that a note has also been placed on the bedside table.

> *Peach,*
>
> *I called your restaurant and spoke to Sophie. She said they can handle things without you, so take all the time you need and don't worry about a thing. I told her you won't be in today at all and she was glad to hear you're taking some time off. She said to remind you that both she and Maddie "have been following your pie recipe perfectly for the past 3 months and it's about time you stopped micro-managing everyone" (direct quote).*
>
> *I'll cook you some food when you're hungry.*
> *Sleep as long as you want.*
> *Max*

That's so nice of him. But I can't take a day off. We're fully booked again today and our pie orders have been insane. I climb out of bed and find the bathroom. I flick on the light.

Wow. It's palatial. There's a walk-in shower with two shower heads. I decide to get in. I peel off my clothes and step into the shower, which does a good job of clearing my head. I dry myself off with one of the super-deluxe towels and put my clothes back on, since I don't have anything else to change into. I open the drawer, looking for toothpaste, and find a packaged new toothbrush, toothpaste, a comb and a hair dryer. By the time I'm done, I almost feel human again.

I feel surprisingly well-rested.

Carefully, I open the door of my bedroom. I could just leave him a note and quietly leave. He's probably busy or at work or something. Then again, he said he was taking some time away from the office after...getting arrested.

"Hey." He's sitting at the marble island in his open-plan kitchen, working on his laptop. He's wearing jeans and a black t-shirt that's sort of hugging every single one of his burly muscles. He's tan and his tattoos give him a bad-boy vibe that's spliced with that dark pirate edge. His hair is lightly pushed back from his face and he looks... good. Okay, more than *good.* Gorgeous would be an understatement. It's hard not to stare.

It's strange to see him in the light of day. His over-the-top tough guy glamor is even more pronounced.

"Hi." I walk over to him, a little awkwardly. I'm

surprised to see that, outside the open wall of his apartment, where the blue water of his pool is sparkling and the palm trees are gently swaying, it's a beautiful day. "What time is it?"

"A little after six."

"I better go help with the pies. But I just want to say I really appre—"

"Six at night."

"At *night?*"

"You slept for sixteen hours."

"What?"

"You must have needed it."

Shit. No wonder I feel so well-rested. I haven't slept like that since before I left Georgia. Or, ever, maybe. "God. I should go and—"

"I've been in touch with Sophie several times. She said to assure you that they've got everything covered. She wants you to take a few days off." He holds out his phone. "Here, call her. There's a charger over there if you want to plug in."

He unlocks his phone and finds Sophie—whose name has already been added to his contacts—in his list of recent calls. "I had to assure her I didn't kidnap you and that I'm not a serial killer. She's been calling every couple of hours to check on you."

Sophie picks up on the first ring. "Max?" she says.

"It's Peach."

"Peach. Jesus. First of all, are you okay?"

"I just slept for sixteen hours straight."

"I'm not surprised. Second, the 'friend' you ran into is *Max freaking Black*? Why didn't you tell me you're friends with him?"

"You know him?"

Max glances up at me and blinks, which makes my stomach do that fluttery thing again. He's just ridiculously beautiful. There's no other word for it.

"I don't *know* him," Sophie says. "I know *of* him, though, of course. Everyone does. He's basically the hottest freaking guy in L.A.! Also one of the most promiscuous and also under house arrest, just saying. Which of course can all be overlooked when it's Max Black we're talking about. When can I meet him? God, Peach, are you *sleeping wi*—?"

"No. And I'm headed down there now."

"You absolutely are *not*! You're taking tonight off. And tomorrow. Otherwise your staff will mutiny. We've all seen the stress you've been under and how exhausted you've been. We can handle it, I promise. We don't need you here tonight. All hands are on deck and everything is running like clockwork."

"Are you sure?" It *would* be nice to have a night off. I feel well-rested, but also like I could crawl back into that king-sized bed and sleep for another sixteen hours.

"Johnny's ordering you to stay away. Plus, since it's Max Black you're hanging out with, it would basically be criminal—no pun intended—not to ride that train all the way to the station, if you know what I mean. We don't want to see your face around here until Tuesday morning. Am I making myself clear enough?"

"What day is it?" My sense of time feels skewed.

"It's Saturday night, Peach." Her tone is exasperated. "Tomorrow's Sunday, which you're also taking off. We're closed on Mondays. You can come back to work on Tuesday. Okay?"

I relent. "All right. If you're sure."

"I'm sure. And I want to meet Max at our very next opportunity."

"I'll see what I can do." Not that I'm going to be seeing Max again after…*this*, whatever this actually is—or introducing him to anyone.

After I end the call, I realize that, if I'm not going back to work, then I'm not going back to my closet-sized office. Which is also my bedroom.

As though reading my thoughts, Max says, "So it's all decided. You'll stay here until Tuesday morning."

"You could hear all that?"

"Yeah. She was kind of yelling. She also told me all that stuff the last couple of times I talked to her. Except for the part about pointing out that I'm a criminal."

I can't help smiling at him, a little guiltily. Because he would have heard all that other stuff, too, about how hot he is. Which is accurate, not that I'm going to mention any of that, of course.

"Would you like coffee?" he says. "Or champagne? We could finish that bottle we opened last night."

As appealing as spending the evening drinking champagne with Max Black in his to-die-for apartment might be, I'm still not sure I belong here. He must have other things to do besides babysit me. "I don't want to impose on you, Max. I appreciate you offering me a bed for the night, but I think it's best if——"

"Please," he says. "I'm on lock down, I've got this huge apartment all to myself, I'm tired of spending all my time alone, and I've got an open bottle of champagne I really don't want to drink by myself. You can't tell me no." The look he gives me is equal parts mischievous and heart-breaking. Because the shadows under his eyes are just as pronounced as they were that day he came into the restaurant.

He's suffered, somewhere along the line, and it shows. *He's lonely.*

"I bought some things and had them delivered," he says. "When I thought you might stay a few more days."

"What things?"

He motions toward a row of shopping bags that have been set against the wall. There are at least a dozen of them. "A change of clothes and a few other things. In case you want to swim."

"You bought me...clothes?"

"I didn't want you to feel like you had to go back to work or your office if you didn't need to."

I don't know whether to be offended or flattered. It might be the most considerate thing anyone has ever done for me. Grandma Bea isn't one for frivolous gestures. She's staunch and matter-of-fact and gets on with things. She doesn't have the money to spend on trinkets or gifts. Birthdays meant a hand-made card with a twenty dollar bill inside and maybe a new pie plate or a whisk or a wooden spoon, if I was lucky.

"I got a bunch of different sizes because I wasn't exactly sure."

"Max. You really didn't have to do that."

"I know." He takes a swig of his beer. The way he says it is smug and laced with an uncut masculinity that reminds me of how he protected me. How he's protecting me now. He doesn't want me to have to leave the safety of his apartment until I want to. Until I'm ready to face the very real danger that's become a part of my reality.

"Thank you."

"You're welcome. Now, how about that champagne?"

So I'm staying with Max Black for another night, it seems. And possibly even tomorrow night and the night after that.

It's a strange turn of events, but now that I'm here, I decide to go with it, at least for tonight. I trust him, even though I'm still not entirely sure why I would. He's nice.

He pours us some champagne and clinks his glass against mine.

Our gazes meet as we sip our drinks. "Let's sit outside," he says.

He grabs the bottle and I follow him out past his hot tub and pool to a seating area with luxury couches and a stunning view of the city. He disappears inside again and comes out with two huge platters of food. "I ordered these a few hours ago. I figured you'd be hungry when you woke up."

As a matter of fact, I'm starving. There's cheese and fancy crackers and thin-sliced beef and salmon and olives and delicious dips.

"I called the cops to see if there's been any sign of the stalker," Max says. "They've been patrolling the area but they haven't been able to locate him."

"Oh."

"Sorry to bring it up, but I thought you might want to know."

"They told me a restraining order doesn't work unless you have a bodyguard on call 24/7."

"That's true." He takes another sip of his drink. "I know this might sound strange, Peach, but I'd like you to let me do that for you."

"Do what for me?"

"Be your bodyguard. Just for the time being."

I can't believe he would offer such a thing. "I'm sure you have other things to worry about besides me and my psycho-drama."

"To tell you the truth, I've been going a little stir crazy

since I've been under house arrest. It'll give me something to do. It'll take my mind off my own problems. Please. It's a win-win."

I stare at him for a few seconds. It's basically like staring at the sun. His thick hair curls lightly over his collar. The rough stubble of his day-old beard is ridiculously…masculine. His face is stunningly, ruggedly handsome. His eyes are sapphire, like blue embers. His body is long and lean and absurdly toned.

As I drink in all the details of him, an unexpected decision comes to me.

If they don't catch the stalker, I'll probably end up going back to Georgia, and soon. I can't live here in L.A. if it means I have to be terrified, restaurant or no restaurant. *Beefed-up bodyguard or no beefed-up bodyguard.* I'll go home and do my best to make a life for myself that's less about aspirations and more about settling into safety and comfort and familiarity. I'm tough but I'm not tough enough to defy threats of physical bodily harm or worse.

But I'm not ready to go just yet.

I swore off men because I was scared I'd get my heart broken. Which is a stupid thing to do, come to think of it. Replacing pain with nothingness is hardly going to be a satisfying life plan. All of a sudden, I'm done worrying about it. Getting stalked and attacked by a psychotic stranger will do that to a person, I guess. It changes your perspective.

I'm paying too high a price for my mother's loss, is what I'm realizing.

What I'm also realizing is that I no longer care if I get my heart broken. At least I'll feel *something*. At least it'll be me living my life instead burying my head in the sand by working so hard I never have time to look up.

Something about Max Black makes me *want* to feel things. Maybe because his own heartbreak—or whatever it is that haunts him—is so close to the surface. I'm pretty sure that, whatever I end up *feeling* with Maximillian Apollo Black, if I get that far, will be the most profound thing that's ever happened to me. You can just tell. By the dark look in his eyes.

If I have to give up my dream, there's one thing I want to do first.

One burly, blue-eyed thing who has not only saved me once, but now is offering to save me as many times as I need to be saved.

I'm a 21-year-old virgin, because I'm a fool, that's why. Because I was scared of getting hurt.

The events of the past few weeks have clarified something: I'm going to get hurt anyway. So I might as well experience some of the highs and lows along with the middles, which is where I feel like I've pretty much lived my entire life: right there in the goddamn middle, avoiding pain and, in the process, avoiding the good stuff too. The star-struck this and the head over heels that.

Even if it leaves you cold, at least you've touched fire along the way.

He seems like a good person, he's hot AF, he's my chaperone for the next two days and we're locked away together in his plush penthouse. What I'm going to do before I run back to Georgia is to experience something most girls my age have been rolling around in for years by this point.

Hot, take-no-prisoners sex.

Give me a high, Max Black, I want to say. Make me *feel.*

I've got two days to see if I can somehow convince him to enlighten me and show me all the things I've been missing out on. I don't have the first clue how to do this.

I wonder if I can.

7

THE CHAMPAGNE IS AFFECTING HER, maybe, or the night. I like the city at dusk. The thick air and the pinks and oranges of the sky. It paints her hair an even more spectacular color. She's dazzling me, like she did that first time, as though her body and soul are glittering with stardust.

And here I go again. *Calm down, man. You've already decided that this is a business arrangement. You know you'd hurt her and fuck up her life with your twisted mess of a personality. You don't do relationships. You don't know how. The only thing you know how to do is to use women and break them. Like you've done so many times before.*

Or maybe not. Maybe I could learn how to be a better person.

Yeah, right. She's way too good for you. You're a hopeless wretch. You'll only dirty her beautiful purity. Don't delude yourself into thinking you can change.

She's relaxed a little. She seems to have accepted that she's staying with me again tonight. I can feel my own heartbeat and it's heavy and hot.

"I wonder where he is right now," she says, and I know who she's talking about. Her stalker.

The rage inside me is jagged, like small, pointed knives of fury. "We'll catch him, don't worry." It's already decided. I'll kill or die, or both, to protect her. *That's* how I can prove to her that a small part of me is worthy of her. It sounds fucked up, and it is, but it's already become who I am now. I've finally found my purpose and here it is.

"Let's just let the police handle it, Max."

My name, spoken like that in her angel's voice, kills me a little more. I love the sound of it, like a soothing tonic to my battered psyche.

She's watching me. A little connection between us is forming. The intensity of my reaction to her is almost disorienting. So I steer the conversation in a different direction. I top up her glass. "Tell me about Georgia."

She smiles. "You want to hear about Georgia?"

"Yeah. Your family's there?"

"My father died when I was four. My mother died a few years later. In a skiing accident."

"I'm sorry to hear that. My parents died when I was young, too."

"Really? I'm sorry, Max."

"It was a long time ago. Tell me more."

She's watching me, like she thinks it's intriguing that I want to hear about her life, but she gives me what I want. More. Of anything she's willing to give. "I went to live with my grandmother after they died. She still lives in the house I grew up in. It's a big old rambling plantation house. It needs a lot of work. I was hoping to fix it up for her if the business became successful. Hopefully I'll still be able to do that. You'd like her," she adds. The way she says this makes me feel, I don't know, borderline emotional. That she would consider who I would like or not like.

And it's the strangest thing: I want to meet her grandmother.

I could send contractors. I could get them to do everything her grandmother tells them to do, exactly the way she wants it. Is it too soon?

Just sitting here next to Peach, listening to her talk as we drink champagne, watching her eyes sparkle when she smiles, it's where I want to be. I can't remember ever feeling this way: content to be exactly where I am in the moment. It feels so foreign, so *good*.

"Grandma Bea taught me how to cook and bake and, well, everything else," she says. "She lent me the money to start the business. I'll still pay her back. It just might take a little longer."

"You'll still be able to. I'm not going to let that asshole

de-rail your plans, Peach. No way." Our eyes meet. I feel light-headed from her beauty and its stunning, savage power over me.

Her eyes are so blue, so clear. "Max. Please. I don't want you doing anything that might get you arrested… again."

I let myself bask in some of her influence as she smiles gently. And I feel the hard heart of me soften the smallest bit, like she's shining her light into the darkest corners of me.

All those women from my jaded past who tried to convince me of things I never believed: none of them ever got close. And then *this* happens…this little golden goddess swans into my life and slays me, with no effort at all. A blink of those long, copper-tinted eyelashes in my direction and that's all it takes. I've basically been reduced to a mess of infatuation.

It's quite possible that I've felt more happiness in the few hours I've spent with her than in the rest of all my twenty-four years combined. Ridiculous but true. Happiness is not an emotion I've had a lot of experience with. My mother died when I was four. My father died when I was seven. Rafe raised me and did the best he could, but it was hard. He was driven to succeed so he could get us out of the poverty we found ourselves mired in and it took its toll. We struggled. And I mean we fucking *struggled*. We had nothing. We lived in a shack because we had no other choice. We were hungry all the time. He was forced to leave me alone so he could go to school and get good grades and also work to try to get the money we so desperately needed. He didn't know how all that would turn out until it was too late. *How leaving me alone would make me vulnerable to the twisted agenda of the one person who was supposed to have cared about us...how it would force me to fight back...*

But that's a story best left alone.

So I promise her this, hoping I can keep that promise before I even say it. "I'll do my best not to get arrested. But he'll come back. And I'm going to be waiting for him when he does. In the meantime, I'll watch over you." I realize what I sound like and I don't want her to think I'm walking some kind of lunatic line. So I try to tone it down. "I can work from the restaurant. You can find me a quiet corner and no one will even know I'm there. Just for a while."

She's watching me and there are layers to her expression. She's not sure why I would offer such a thing. She's grateful but guarded. Then I notice that her eyes are shiny with tears.

I can't handle this at all. My reactions to her are so new to me. I carefully smooth a strand of her hair from her damp cheek. I wipe her tears with my fingers. I hardly recognize myself. I don't *do* tender and caring. Or at least I never have until now.

"Everything's going to be okay," I tell her. "It's scary, I know. But you'll be fine. I'm here now."

"Why are you doing this for me?"

"Because you're letting me." It's a slightly odd thing to say, maybe, but I'm not myself tonight.

She sniffs. "I just don't want you to get hurt or in trouble, Max. It's not worth it."

"Of course it's worth it."

"You don't need to get involved in all this. Really."

"I'm already involved." *I'm more than involved. I'm so fucking involved it's all I care about. It's the only thing that actually means anything to me.*

"I'm not usually the kind of girl who needs to be saved," she says.

"I'm not usually the kind of guy who does the saving."

You hear about these things happening, like in those corny movies where someone meets someone else and the entire course of their life is transformed, just like that, off onto some entirely new trajectory. That's what it's like.

I've turned a corner, and the landscape is new and unfamiliar and wildly beautiful. All I want to do is keep going.

"You wait right here," I tell her. "I got some things for you." I go in and grab the shopping bags and carry them out to her.

She wipes her eyes and laughs lightly. "I can't believe you bought me all this."

They're even wrapped, like presents. I vaguely remember being asked if I wanted the purchases gift wrapped and I'd gruffly agreed. Now I'm glad. I only wish I'd bought her more. I hand her the first bag. "Open it."

It's a light blue silk dress that almost matches the color of her eyes.

Now it feels slightly awkward, to have bought her clothes, but she holds up the dress. "It's cute, Max. I like it. But I still don't know why you've done all this."

"I told them my guest needed some things but I wasn't sure what size. I tried to describe you. And I asked them to send more than one of each. Hopefully some of this stuff fits."

She glances at me, a hint of mischief touching her expression. "How did you describe me?"

"I said nothing they could bring me would be as beautiful as you are but they should try anyway." I smile at her, like I'm joking.

She shakes her head a little and opens the next one. She holds up two tiny shreds of animal print fabric. She laughs. "Wow."

"I asked them to send a few different styles because I wasn't sure what you liked."

There are two one-piece suits and three more bikinis. There are shirts, sweaters, more dresses, underwear, socks, pajamas, and a coat. "Max. This is way too much. You really didn't need to do all this."

I don't say what I'm thinking: *now you don't have to leave. You have everything you need right here.*

"It's a nice night," she says. "I guess I could try out one of these new bathing suits. We could sit in the hot tub."

After all this, I'm wondering if it's a good idea. Just the thought ignites something voracious in me. I've already admitted to myself that I'm mildly—okay, more than *mildly*—intrigued by Peach Sutton. Okay, more than *intrigued*. I've also decided she's strictly off limits. My role is to keep her safe from a deviant. Not to give in to my *own* deviance, which is probably equal to that of the fucker who's stalking her.

My problem is, she's so fucking gorgeous it's distracting me.

As she holds up another bikini—a minuscule white one—I can't help but picture her in it, *with only a few shreds of flimsy fabric covering her perfect—*

No.

My cock, which is suffering from some serious withdrawal, gets instantly and painfully rock hard. I can only thank fuck it's practically dark out now because I've suddenly got ten inches of hot, raging lust to contend with and I don't want to scare her or fucking freak her out.

It's not a good idea. "I, uh…" I hold up my wrist,

where my metal cuff is firmly attached. "I can't get this wet. But you go ahead."

"No," she says. "I don't want to, alone. I'll probably have an early night. I'm still pretty tired."

The thought of her leaving me, even to go to bed, is surprisingly difficult to bear. *Am I losing my mind?* Possibly, because I hear myself say, "I guess I could just hold it over the edge."

She looks up at me and—*holy hell*—I'm such a goner.

She's so damn *pretty*. So sweet and sexy and mouth-watering. I want to devour her. I want to taste every inch of her. I want to lick her and hold her down and make her moan with ecstasy.

I won't.

It'll be the purest form of torture, but I'll sit there in that goddamn hot tub next to her sweet, wet body and I won't touch.

One thing I do know: resisting her is going to be the hardest thing I've ever had to do in my life.

As Peach is getting changed, I throw on some swim shorts and get into the hot tub. I turn on the jets. At least the bubbles will hide the fact that my hard-on is a beast of pulsing fucking agony. Usually, at a time like this, I'd go pump iron like a maniac for three hours until all the rage and lust and angst was worked out of my system. Now, the torment rages. It's painful. Existentially painful, more than anything. It's lust with an edge, like *this* lust is only the tip of some huge, unknowable iceberg. Again, new territory. Georgia Peach territory. So exquisite you think you might die of the overload.

You can look but not touch.

You can fantasize but not act on it.

And here she comes. Walking toward me with a towel wrapped around her. Which she drops, and the minute she does, I know this was all a terrible mistake.

The tiny white bikini hugs her curves like a second skin.

Her body.

Fucking hell.

Her breasts are full and unbelievably beautiful and straining against the tight shreds of fabric. I can clearly see the outline of her taut nipples. My mouth literally waters. Her stomach is flat but not in a washboard abs kind of way, but more of a natural, feminine way that blows my mind for some reason. Her hips flare gently and her legs are long and perfectly shaped.

She's *stunning.*

A blush rises to her cheeks when she glances at me and sees the look on my face—which I try to tone down —as she lowers herself into the hot tub. "This is nice," she says, leaning against the side, facing me.

Nice. It's a lot more than *nice.* It's a moment in time I'll never forget. Because as I watch her from this small distance, noticing the soft curl of her hair, the swell of her breasts, the shape of her mouth, I'm realizing that I'm no longer the person I was. I'll keep this little stranger safe but it's not the only thing I'm going to do. *I'm in love*, simple as that.

This is a fucking problem. I *can't* be in love. I don't know *how* to love. It feels strange, like I've just had a blood transfusion and been given a completely different variety. It's hotter, and kinder. It's steering my thoughts in unchartered directions. Like how the fuck I'm going to navigate being the man she needs when I'm actually the man I am? Dark. Damaged. Fucked way the hell up.

Maybe I'm overdramatizing the extent of my issues. Maybe I'm fine. Maybe I'll cruise into a relationship like any other mild-mannered prick would, and live happily ever after.

Don't fucking delude yourself, Max. You'll systematically ruin her life. It's what you do.

Fuck off, I say to the voice in my head. That's not the only possibility. Maybe I *can* do it. Maybe I can dig deeper than I ever have before.

"Yeah," I say, even though I'm devastated. By the choice I have to make. I can risk hurting her, which I inevitably will. Or I can hire bodyguards to protect her and walk away.

8

Okay, so now what?

We're in the hot tub, both leaning against opposite sides. Max has his burly arm resting along the top, to keep his bracelet from getting wet. He's up to his neck but I can see some of his tattoos a little more clearly now. One is of a dragon. There's an eagle, too, and some intricate tribal-type designs. I wonder what they mean.

I notice, too, that he has some scars on his chest and his shoulders. Small, crescent-shaped cuts, long healed over. What would cause something like that?

His shoulders and his chest are…very impressively built, to say the least. He must work out *a lot.*

I don't really know how to read him. He's gone quiet. Is that a good sign or a bad one?

Damn it. Now I wish I hadn't been such a prude all

these years, and so distracted. I don't know the first thing about how to seduce a man.

It can't be that hard, though, right?

Am I brave enough?

It's nerve-wracking. He's so freaking *built*. And sort of moody. He seems like he's conflicted about something.

I could move closer. I could say something. The last genius pronouncement I'd come up with was *this is nice*.

What can I say that might break the ice that's suddenly plunged us into silence?

It's warm for October. He doesn't want to talk about the weather, you idiot.

I like your hot tub. No kidding. That's why you're *in* it.

What's the significance of the dragon? It doesn't *need* significance. It looks cool, that's enough significance.

What are those scars from? That's entirely none of your business.

Put me in a hot tub with one inked-up, drop-dead gorgeous hunk and my brain turns to mush.

Before I can even start to make a plan about how I might begin to—how did Sophie put it?...*ride that train all the way to the station*...Max's phone starts ringing. It's sitting on the ledge next to the hot tub, within easy reach. He checks the number. "Do you mind if I take this? It's my business colleague who's been checking some leads about the hacking of my laptop."

"Go right ahead."

He presses the speaker button. "Hey, Mike."

"There was a breach into your email account," the guy says, "and a virus was downloaded by opening one of the emails. I'm not sure which one yet, though. It's encrypted. I also found some surveillance footage. Someone broke into your office."

"Who?"

"Can't tell. But it looks like…a woman."

"A *woman*? Who is it?"

"I don't know, Max. She's wearing a hood and it's hard to make out much detail. Looks like she has dark hair, though. How many women with dark hair have a vendetta against you?"

"Too many to count," Max says, and I wonder what he means by that. Why would they have vendettas against him?

"I think you should see this. What are you doing right now? I could bring it over. I've just left the office. I'm right around the corner."

Max glances at me. "Do you mind?"

"Of course not." I'm not sure I'm up for a big seduction scene tonight, anyway. I'm realizing how pathetic I am, and it's not a great feeling. Maybe it's too late for me. Maybe I've already let too much of life pass me by. Maybe I'm a hopeless case. I mean, I *hope* I'm not but it's hard not to wonder, when you're twenty-one years old and have no idea how to be sexy or seductive and in fact have barely even *kissed* a boy. Plenty have tried, but I was a fast runner and good at climbing trees. And I was even better at hiding myself away in my grandmother's big kitchen, baking up a storm while covered in flour and surrounded by four meddling and very observant and outspoken old women.

"See you soon, then." Max ends the call. "This won't take long," he says to me.

"It's fine, Max. I'd definitely want to know who broke in to my office, if it was me."

There's a banging on the door. Max stands up and grabs a towel, wrapping it around his waist.

And…holy hell.

He's…there's…an enormous *swell* in his shorts that's…*Jesus H….huge.*

Dauntingly and gigantically…*hard.*

Could that be…*because of me?*

Goddamn it! Why did I wait so long to find out about all this stuff?

If I was only a little more worldly I'd know what to do. I'd know how to handle this.

As it is, Max walks over to the door to open it and his friend comes out to the patio, along with Max, who still has the thick towel wrapped around him. At this point it's doing a good job of hiding … *it* and I try not to stare.

"Peach, this is Mike Finch. Mike, Peach. Excuse me while I go throw on some jeans."

"Hey, Peach," says Mike, and he sort of stares at me, but then again I'm in the hot tub so maybe that's just a thing that happens when you're sitting in a hot tub being introduced to a finance geek who's fully clothed, who would know?

"Hi."

Mike sets up his laptop on the table and Max returns, wearing jeans and a t-shirt. While they're distracted, I try to subtly raise myself out of the hot tub, grab a towel and wrap it around myself. As I do this, though, Max's attention is diverted from the computer screen to…me, and as he watches me, his gaze turns dark. Even though I sometimes find him hard to read, *this* look isn't hard to read at all. It's hot and sort of feral and just about the sexiest thing that's ever happened to me.

Yikes.

"See?" Mike is saying, and Max looks away again to watch the video.

"Shit," says Max. "It's Melanie. Fucking hell. *She's* the hacker?"

"Who's Melanie?" says Mike. "One of your exes?"

"I'd hardly call her an ex. Can you trace the virus? Was that her, too?"

"We haven't figured out how to track the source of it. As I said, it's encrypted."

"*She's* the one who framed me?"

"If she's breaking into your office in dark clothes and a hood, then my guess is it's pretty likely."

I leave them to it and go into the open plan living room to find my phone, which is now recharged. I sit on the couch and check my messages. There are a few from

Sophie. And one from Grandma Bea. *Miss you, darlin. Hope you're having fun in the big city.*

I smile. I taught Grandma Bea and her friends how to use Snapchat and now they send me pictures of the four of them. Playing bridge. Drinking gin. There's one of the peach orchard, which makes my throat feel tight. All the peaches have been harvested by now, but I love it there in the fall.

I check my emails and the restaurant's Instagram, which has two thousand new followers. This couch is so comfortable and my eyes feel so heavy and I decide I'll just close them for a minute until Max is finished.

I dream of the peach orchard. In my dream, I'm not alone.

Max is there with me.

I wake with a start.

What was that noise?

My heart is racing.

I'm back in my bed in Max's guest room and the towel I'd wrapped around myself has been draped over a chair. I'm still wearing my bikini.

He carried me to bed again. He unwrapped the towel and tucked me in.

Did he look at me? What was he thinking about? Was he—

I hear another noise. Someone's groaning.

Who is it?

I climb out of bed and tiptoe into the living room.

The sound is coming from Max's room.

Is he with someone?

But then I hear him moan again. It's a deep, anguished sound. A tormented sound.

The door of his room is open.

I see him there, asleep on his bed. He's lying on top of the duvet, wearing only a pair of boxers. He moans in that agonized way again and stirs a little.

"Max?" I whisper from the door. He's restless in his sleep. He moans again. It sounds like the word *no*. Like he's having a terrible dream.

I take a step closer. His dream only seems to be getting deeper, and worse.

I'm standing close to the bed. I'm not sure how to wake him. I realize I'm still dressed only in my bikini. Should I go and put—

He groans again, louder this time. It's such a pained sound, and angry, too. There are shades of fury and terror and sadness.

"Max," I whisper again. "It's okay. It's just a dream."

He goes still for a few seconds.

His face is stunning in the low light. Dark lashes lay in graceful arcs against his cheeks. His nose has been broken and there are two small scars, one on the bridge of his nose, the other on his cheekbone. Poor Max. He seems so battered by life. His lips are perfect. He hasn't shaved in a day or two and the stubble of his beard is dark and coarse. His neck is corded and strong-looking. A tiny pulse plays at the base of his throat. His broad, muscular shoulders are decorated with those elaborate inked designs. His hair-dusted skin is the color of rosewood. A gold chain hangs around his neck, catching sparked light.

And there, the scars. Small, silver crescents. *What are they?*

He groans again.

Very gently, I lean closer. I don't want to scare him. I touch his shoulder. "Max?" I whisper. "Everything's okay." My fingers, feather-light, graze across one his scars.

Max's eyes open but they're blank. Just completely empty of expression. He grabs me and before I can think or react, I'm on his bed. With his big body on top of me.

The iron grip of his strong hands closes around my neck.

9

THE HOT WIND rattles at the loose iron of the shack's flimsy roof. Rain plinks onto the iron like tiny marbles. A single candle burns low in its glass jar, my only light. I know how to make sure it won't catch the place on fire. Keep it right in the middle of the wooden table, Rafe said. He won't be back until late. He's at work at the surf shop two blocks away. I'm not allowed there ever since I knocked over all those surfboards. It wasn't even my fault. He'll get fired if I sneak in and hide in the back room again like I did last week. I didn't mean to melt all that wax with the lighter. It was just sitting there. I thought I could help. If he loses his job, he said, we won't have money to buy food.

So I have to stay here.

I ate the sandwich he made me. I'm still hungry.

I'm lonely. The batteries for the radio are dead. There's no phone and no one to call anyway.

A door slams in the distance and the sound makes me jump.

I'm scared.

Rafe, come home. Please come home.

I blow out the candle. Maybe the darkness will hide me.

I know better than to bolt the door. He'll cut me again. Hurt me worse.

I sit in the farthest, darkest corner, on the floor. He said he'd kill Rafe if I run. I'm going to kill him, if I can. It's the only way to stop him.

I can hear his footsteps. Swearing. The howl of the wind.

The door flies open, banging loud.

I try to make myself small and invisible. I try so hard to disappear. To sink through the floor, to obliterate myself into a black hole that never ends.

"Come here, boy."

I don't answer. Maybe he won't find me. I'm in the corner, in the dark.

A glint of light flashes off the blade of his knife.

I'm holding a knife, too. It's the one I found at the surf shop. Big one, too. I hope Rafe doesn't get fired because I stole it but it was worth the risk. I need it.

He finds me.

No.

He yanks on my arm.

No.

I can't bear it. I jab the knife. It sinks into him so very easily. Just slides right on in, deeply, at the side of his lower back. All the way to the hilt.

He makes a strangled sound. Of gurgling, horrible surprise.

Finally, I have enough strength to push him away. The rage rises and overflows. I lash out, gripping with my hands.

Instantly, I know something's wrong. I can feel the terror fall away as reality shifts. As sleep fades out and I realize I'm a million miles from that dank little beach shack and that horrific dark night.

My grasp loosens. My eyes focus.

Peach.

My hands drop away, scalded by what I've just done. I jump up. Off of her.

I was on her. I was pinning her down.

I sit heavily against the far wall, keeping my distance. My heart is hammering in my chest.

I swore I would never hurt her, and already, I have. "I'm sorry," I start to gasp. "I'm sorry."

The blue of her eyes is bright, even in the darkness. There's fear there, which kills me more than I can handle. I grab my hair in my fist. If I could cry I would but my tears dried up a long time ago, forged by the fury that never quite leaves me.

Her copper-gold hair catches light in the dim room. She is quite simply the most stunning creature I've ever seen or imagined. The skin of her neck where my hands held her is pink. *You fucking bastard.* You're *the one she needs protection from, you fucked-up freak.*

She gets up off the bed. The sight of her in that bikini is literally destroying me. Her curves are sweet and perfect and mind-numbing. I love everything about her. And I almost just killed her.

I wait for her to walk out, to distance herself as much as she can from me and my lunatic tendencies. I've ruined everything. I've destroyed the best thing that ever happened to me, just like I've destroyed everything else. I don't know why I expected this to be different. I don't know why I thought I might be capable of redemption. I always knew I was a lost cause.

She doesn't walk out.

She comes closer. She sits next to me on the floor. I resist both of my violent urges: to move away and also to move closer.

"You didn't hurt me, Max," she says in her angel's voice. "Not at all."

I can barely speak. "I *strangled* you."

"Not really. You woke up right away. I shouldn't have touched you like that. I knew you were having a nightmare. I scared you."

She's blaming *herself*? "Peach, listen. I'm…messed up. You should know that about me. If you want me to leave, I will. You can stay here as long as you want. You can have it."

"Have it?"

"Everything."

She smiles, but her eyes are sad. "Max, I don't want you to leave." Very quietly, she asks, "Who hurt you? Someone hurt you."

I've talked about all this shit in therapy, from time to time, although I hardly ever went. And to Rafe, over the years. It never made much of a difference. The last thing I want to do is spill my guts to this golden little angel, but the way she's looking at me, searchingly and with total, soft-edged empathy…it feels like she's drawing it out of me. She wants to know. And I want to give her everything she wants. It's difficult to do, though. Confessing the wreckage of my past always feels like reaching into my chest and pulling my heart out by its bloody roots. "It was a long time ago."

Very gently, she reaches up and starts to unclench my fist from my hair.

All I want to do is be so careful with her that she'll find a way to forgive me. I let her do whatever she wants to me. I let her take my hand and hold it.

"I'm sorry I scared you," she says. "I'll know better next time."

Next time.

I look into her eyes and all I can do is hope. She's so damn pretty.

She tugs on my hand. "Come on. Get up. Come with me."

I don't have it in me to refuse her. I get up and let her lead me back to bed. "Lie down," she orders me.

I do.

"Do you want me to stay with you for a little while, Max?"

"Yes." *No. Let her go. Let her walk away.*

She lays down next to me. Her presence feels so good, so calming.

I don't dare to think about the rest of it. Her outrageous beauty. Her skin and her body and that damn bikini. I look over at her and I concentrate on her eyes. How blue they are. How they're my exact favorite color.

I turn on my side, to face her. She lays on her side, too.

So we're lying there in the warm, dark room, face to face, a few feet apart. It's peaceful and connective and I'm so in the moment I can almost cast off the memories for a while. I'm here, now, with her. That's all that matters to me.

"When did it happen?" she says.

A manageable question. "When I was eleven."

"Who was it?"

More difficult, but I tell her anyway. "My uncle. My father's older half-brother who he hadn't even spoken to in twenty years. No wonder." And now that I've started, I keep going. "I killed him. I stabbed him with a knife."

She gasps lightly. "What?"

"Yeah. I've killed a man. It's okay if you never want to see me again. I'd understand. It's the worst thing I've ever done but I had a good reason." I'm a little flummoxed that I'd admit all that, so easily, so quickly.

I expect her to be disgusted. To run. She doesn't. She

doesn't move, or say anything for a while. She's watching my face as I watch hers.

"What was the reason?" she says softly.

A harder question. But here in this dark room with her soft perfection, so careful with everything about me, I don't mind. I can give her something of myself I so rarely give. "He was a predator. He used to cut me. Some twisted thrill, I guess. He threatened to do more than that and to kill my brother if I told or if I ran. I wasn't willing to give in to his demands. And I was trapped. So I fought back."

We lay there quietly for a while as she absorbs this information. "I could have killed that man the other night," she says. "If I hadn't been able to get away, and if I'd been holding a knife, I could have done that."

"I'm glad you didn't have to. It's not something that ever goes away, even when you know you had to do it and it was the only thing you could have done." It's very likely that *I'm* going to kill that man, I know this. He won't go away. It's possible he'll get arrested but even if he does, it won't be for long enough. I'm fully prepared to do whatever needs to be done, to keep her from having to live with such a thing. With fear or violence or with blood on her hands. It's better if I do it. I'm already tainted.

"Max?"

"Yeah?"

"It wasn't your fault. You're a good person."

I exhale a weak laugh. "I just strangled you then told you I killed someone."

"You think you're ruined because of that, but you're not. I can tell. You're good."

"You don't know me very well."

"I can still tell."

This could have almost made me smile if I wasn't so tormented. I look over at her and she's blinding me with her lush, golden gorgeousness. "How?"

"You're kind. You go out of your way to help people."

"I go out of my way to help *you*. But not most people."

"Why me, then?"

Well, let me think about that for a second, Peachie Dixie May, I want to say. *Maybe it's those to-die-for blue eyes and those long lashes, blinking at me. Or those ridiculously cute freckles. Or that sweet pink mouth. Or the way being around you makes me feel like I* am *a good person, despite everything.* "Must have been the pies."

She smiles and—*fucking hell*—I'm such a goner. A besotted mess—who can't have the one person I've ever truly wanted, because I don't want to drag her down into the twisted quagmire of my damages, which are so much a part of me.

"Max?"

"Yeah?"

"Can I kiss you?"

Fuck. Can I handle this? "I really don't know why you'd want to."

"You surprised me, when you jumped on me like that. But I wasn't scared of you. Before I could be scared, you'd already jumped off. And I could see it wasn't *you* doing it. I could see it was something else. Something you didn't want."

I blink at her, devastated. I've never stayed in bed with a woman all night or actually slept with anyone. Because of the exact fear that's just been realized. What if I do it again?

"What are you thinking right now?" she says.

"That you should run as far from me as fast as you can."

"Because you killed a predator when you were eleven years old to save yourself?"

"Yes."

"That would be like you running away from me because I kneed that guy where it counts the other night when he attacked me. Sometimes we have to do whatever it takes to survive."

"You're very understanding, but it's not quite the same thing."

"It *is* the same thing. It's exactly the same thing. You're being too hard on yourself."

I don't even know how to respond to that. Except that maybe she's right. Maybe it's time to forgive myself. Problem is, I don't know how.

She twirls an end ringlet of her long hair around one finger and I watch her do this, mesmerized. "I realized something the other day," she says.

"What's that?"

"My mother killed herself because she couldn't live without my father. She loved him so much but then she lost him and she just couldn't take that."

"I'm sorry, Peach."

"And because of that, I swore off getting involved with anyone. For a long time."

"I can see why you would."

"But the thing I realized is that it's too big a price to pay. I'm living a life that's totally empty because I've never let myself feel anything. Because I've been scared to."

"I can probably relate to some of that."

"Have you ever been in love, Max?"

"No." *Actually, yes. As of right now. Or yesterday. Or two weeks ago, to be precise, as crazy as it is.*

She looks at me, almost shyly. "I've never even really kissed anyone."

"I've never even really kissed anyone, either."

Peach smiles and makes an ironic face. "Somehow I find that hard to believe. That the 'hottest man in L.A. and also the most promiscuous,' according to Sophie, has never been kissed."

"I've been with a lot of women," I admit. "But not for a while. And I never kissed any of them."

She absorbs this information, and it already feels like

there's a thread of…not jealousy, but connectivity. *They meant nothing. They were practice for what I'm about to do to you.* It would sound way too cheesy to say it, and I have no idea where this connection will lead yet, because a part of me still wants her to run from me, to keep herself sunny and pure and untouched by the likes of me, even though I know I'd chase after her, because I'm too far gone. "Really?" she says.

"Really."

"Why not?"

"It felt too…intimate. It felt like giving too much. I didn't kiss them and I didn't let them touch me. I never have."

She's quiet for a few seconds. "Ever?"

"Ever."

"It sounds like you've paid too high a price, too, Max. Because of what happened to you."

"Maybe."

"You're hiding pieces of yourself. Like I've been hiding."

"Yeah. Hiding, and shielding." I've never had a conversation like this. I've never been this honest about how I feel.

"Does it…*hurt* when people touch you?"

"It's more of an existential kind of a pain than a physical one."

Another pause. "Would it hurt you if I touched you now?"

"No."

She laughs lightly and my heart is breaking, strangely. Cracking wide open, like little fissures of light and hope are shining into it. "Why not?"

"Because it's you."

She blinks at me and, *holy hell*, she's so damn beautiful. It's the kind of beauty that melts something in you, that stuns you and makes you want to watch her every minute of every day for the rest of time. "What's different about me?"

"You're..." How to say this? "You're the most beautiful person I've ever met. Inside and, well, *outside*. I don't feel like I need to shield myself from you. Not at all."

She seems to take this to heart. She's watching my face like she's emotional about what I've just admitted to her. "What does it feel like when I do this?" Very, very gently, she touches her cool fingers to one of my scars.

I don't even flinch. "It feels like...you're fixing me."

Her eyes get shiny.

"Hey," I say gently.

"My poor Max," she says, as a tear pools and spills down her cheek. I wipe the tear with my finger and—I'm not sure why—I lick it. I have this crazy urge to *take her into myself*. To eat her and drink her and give her everything I have.

Slowly, she leans closer and kisses one of my scars.

I sigh, without meaning to. It's a strange feeling. It's the most forceful thing, and difficult to describe. She's pushing past the boundaries I've always guarded fero-ciously, just with her soft hair and her blue eyes and her sweet lips.

I'm very glad it's dark in here. My cock is so hard and hot and so agonizingly engorged, I know it has escaped the waistband of my boxers, reaching halfway up my stomach. I know it's slick and already starting to spill. I don't want to scare her. But I can't move. And as she kisses another one of the scars on my chest, *fuck*, I think I might be about to come. I groan.

She doesn't pull away. She whispers, "Am I hurting you, Max?"

"No. You're fixing me."

She lays her head on her pillow, closer to mine. "Do you ever wonder what it would be like?"

"What what would be like?"

"A kiss."

"Never until right now. There's only one problem."

"What problem?"

"If I kiss you, I don't think I'll be able to stop kissing you. And I don't want you getting mixed up in all my baggage, Peach. I'm fucked up. I have nightmares every single night. I'm a twisted individual. I always have been. I'm beyond redemption. And I don't want to drag you down with me."

She's watching my eyes. *I love her*, is what I'm thinking. "What if I think you're wrong about all that? Like I was wrong about hiding myself away in the kitchen my entire life because I was too scared to live it?"

"I'd tell you again that you don't know me very well."

"I think I know enough to be able to see that." She leans even closer, but not close enough. She waits there, just watching me.

It's starting to kill me, how much I want her. "Well?" I say.

"Well what?"

"Are you going to kiss me or not?"

"Do you want me to?"

"Most of me does."

"Which part doesn't?"

"The fucked up part."

She feathers a finger across another scar. "We're going to fix that part, remember? So that part doesn't count."

She leans even closer. Very, very softly, she touches her lips to mine. It's overwhelmingly sweet. I touch my tongue to her lips and—*God help me*. She tastes like sugar. Like ripe peaches warmed in the sun. Maybe she absorbed all that from running barefoot through the orchards all her life, living off peach pie and sunshine. "Max?"

"Yeah?"

"You know how I told you I hid myself away because I didn't want to get hurt?"

"Yeah."

"Well, I really did...I'm not very worldly. At all. I've

never actually done…anything. With anyone. So if I don't do it right, just tell me."

I pull back for a second. "You mean you've never had sex?"

"No. I mean, yes, that's what I'm saying. Not even…at all."

I can't help falling for her even more. Not that it would matter, but *hell*. She's never even been touched. She's mine. *Mine.* God, I want her. Forever. I want to be the man she needs, like I've never wanted anything in my wretched life.

"I'm on the pill, though. Grandma Bea insisted that when I left for the big city I should take precautions, just in case. My mother didn't really plan ahead. I was a surprise, I guess you could say. My mother was only eighteen when she had me."

My little Peach is not only dreamily perfect, drop-dead gorgeous, sweet as fuck and wearing a very skimpy bikini in my bed with me, she's also a virgin on the pill who wants a kiss.

I don't have it in me to resist her or refuse her for even a second longer.

I kiss her. I dip my tongue into her mouth and I'm falling falling falling. So damn hard.

I'm a lonely, good-for-nothing sinner who's finally seen God. I'm a love-struck deviant who's finally found a purpose. I'm a fucked-up rebel who finally understands what it means to have something to live for.

10

MAX'S TONGUE touches mine and a warm wave of lust floods my entire body, touching me everywhere.

Oh.

He's so…*hot.* Not just outrageously *hot* hot but also *heat* hot. Being this close to him is *intense.* My body feels like it's humming with soft, sexy warmth.

I blush a little. Lying here in this darkened room with him, half-naked and feeling less alone than I ever have in my life, I'm still aware of my own inexperience.

It *did* scare me when he jumped on me like that, of course it did. But I knew that about him. I knew there was something broken. But not *bad.* Not mean or devious or calculated. The total opposite, in fact. Max's damages are the kind that twist themselves tighter *because* he's a good person. He worries about his darkness. It torments him, where another person might just go with it, or not even care.

His eyes are watching mine and they're so careful, so vividly blue.

Max laughs, softly. And it's the most beautiful, masculine, alluring sound I've ever heard. I feel triumphant. Even after everything we've been through and talked about and confessed, *I've made him happy.* Just a little. It feels like a small triumph. I decide to make it my quest: to make him happy. I have this strangely certain feeling that I *can.* Like maybe it's something *I* can do better than anyone else.

"Well, that was the best thing that ever happened to me, right there."

"The kiss?"

"Yes. The kiss."

He turns his big, buff body toward mine. He props his head up on his bent, muscular arm. He wears a Rolex and a black, beaded bracelet on his right wrist. The combination of the two would look strange on any other businessman but it suits Max, adding to his artistic, pirate-like vibe. His warm, hair-dusted leg rests against my bare skin. His hand smooths a strand of my hair back from my face.

"You're so beautiful, Peach. So perfect."

It's as though he's seeing me like I see him: flawless, despite all the obvious flaws.

We lay there like that for a while, just staring deeply into each other's eyes and it's the most connective experience I've ever had. Like our souls are melting into each other's, merging and entwining.

"Do you trust me?" he says.

"Yes," I whisper.

"You shouldn't."

"I don't care. I do." Everything about him fascinates me. The sculpted shape of his muscular shoulders. The swirling inked designs. His burly chest. My eyes rove down his stomach, to…*Oh. My. God.* In the night-lit darkness I can see the *huge* outline of his hardness, laying taut against his hair-dusted stomach. There's a glimmer there, too, like something about him is wet and somehow *ready*, glistening with his lust. I go shamelessly wet. I can feel a warm, sweet throb soften my most intimate places. My nipples bead against the thin, soft fabric of my bikini top.

After all those years of holding back, now, at the sight of *all* of him, I want him badly. Now. I've become molten and liquid, hot beyond belief.

My fingers touch the ridiculously thick, silky locks of his hair.

His head lowers and warm, sweet anticipation floods into me. His lips graze my cheekbone. Max is kissing me where my bruise was. Softly. "I've wanted to do this from the first second I saw you. I'm going to take such good care of you." Each silky brush of his mouth lights a fiery little channel inside me, igniting me from within. My body comes to life. My breasts feel tender and full, my nipples beaded and aching. Everything about him is so *alluring*.

"Can we do that again?" He blinks those dense lashes.

"You want another kiss?"

"Yes. Yes, I do."

"Okay." I blink at him and he blinks back. He smiles.

Very gently, Max kisses my lips. The kiss turns slippery and greedy. Our bodies entwine. He kisses me again, opening my mouth with his tongue, tasting me, finding intimate angles.

Then, slowly, he pulls back. "You sure about this, Peach?" His deep voice is husky. "I'll give you one last chance to run as far from me as fast as you can. I'd run from *you* if I could, honey, to keep you from getting tangled in my web, but I can't do it."

I can't resist. "Why can't you?"

"First the pies, now the kiss. Everything about you is too damn sweet. I'm already addicted."

My lust is making me bold. "How will you know for sure?"

He smiles. "Maybe if I just taste…a little more of you, then I could make sure."

"Okay, then."

This makes him laugh lightly. Taking his time, he kisses a trail across my shoulder, down the pillowy fullness of my breast. *God.* His fingers graze my nipple, which feels warm and softly electric.

"I'm going to take this off now, sweetheart. I want to taste you. Do you want me to?"

"Yes," I whisper. I'm nervous, but not unsure.

Max seems to have made his decision, like I've made mine. He's sure of himself. He's taking total control.

Max pulls at the ties of my bikini, first the top, then, more slowly, the bottom, and it falls away.

I'm naked.

And I *want* him to see me.

He stares sort of raptly for a few seconds. I started waxing—completely—when I moved to L.A. because someone told me *it was the L.A. thing to do* and I thought I might as well go with it.

I'm flushed and hot and more...*wet* than I've ever been in my life.

Max's eyes are bright but sort of lust-drowsed. "You're so damn gorgeous it hurts," he says.

Am I ready for this?

Max kicks off his boxer shorts and—*Jesus H. Christ.*

"*Max*," I gasp. "How will... ?" I mean, of course I know what goes where but this is ridiculous.

"It'll feel good, trust me. Lay back now."

Oh, God.

Max takes my breasts in his hands. With his fingers, he draws circles around my nipples, teasing them. Then he starts pinching gently, pulling and playing them until each squeeze sends a current of need deep into my body. His mouth kisses my nipple. He licks lightly, teasing, teasing, until it's almost unbearable. He draws the sensitive bud into the hot fire of his mouth and sucks tenderly, increasing the pace and the suction, until a melting warmth starts to build in the core of my body. It feels *so good.* He moves to my other breast, feeding there like he's starving, drawing gently but strongly with his mouth until the melting warmth inside me gets hotter. And deeper. And higher, until it reaches an excruciatingly dazzling peak and then tumbles over it. I moan as the pleasure-surges clench voluptuously inside me, over and over.

Holy hell. Just…wow.

"That's my girl."

"Max," I gasp. "What *was*—?"

He laughs against my breast. "Don't tell me you've never even *come* before. Hell, honey."

I'm *still* sort of *coming*. "I didn't…know…how."

"Shit." He laughs again, biting gently on my nipple until I squirm. "Well, you're about to learn, sugar pie. And you're going to need to get used to it. Because it's official: I *am* addicted. And I haven't even gotten to the best part. Not even close."

Max, I'm learning, is something of a sweet-talker. He's also very, very good at this.

He kisses my breasts again, licking and sucking and taking his time until I think I might be about to come…

again, but then he starts kissing a line down my stomach. His tongue dips into my belly button which makes me squeal but he holds me down and does whatever he wants. He roughly pushes my legs apart and he's kissing lower…until—

"Max?"

"Mmhm?"

"What are you doing?"

He laughs again. "Kissing you."

"But—"

Oh my God.

Max kisses me *there* and I try to roll away from him but he's far too strong. And heavy. And insistent.

"Max, you *can't.*" *Who ever heard of such a thing?* I know I'm unusually naïve about these things but—*oh, God.*

His mouth.

"Just try and stop me." He's not just kissing me, he's *licking* me. Greedily. Hungrily. In slippery, indecent glides. Everywhere. *His tongue is dipping inside me.* "Fuck, you're beautiful," I hear him murmur. "You taste so fucking good."

I feel a slight stretching sensation and almost start to protest but then his mouth fixes onto my clit and starts sucking in deep, gentle draws and I stop protesting. My body goes limp. The pleasure, where his mouth is latched onto me, becomes everything about me. It's centered there, radiating in slow-moving waves. His fingers are using the moisture, sliding inside me, pushing the pleasure deeper, compounding it as the suction of his mouth pulls and pulls in a beautiful rhythm.

He's so *greedy*. So completely *dirty*. One of his fingers slides wetly in a *very* secret place as his other fingers slide deeper inside me and his mouth tugs more strongly until all the sources of pleasure converge in a tidal wave of beauty that shatters me. My pussy clenches tightly around his fingers as he sucks and licks and rubs until it blows my goddamn mind.

I'm writhing against his mouth. Wave after wave of pleasure throbs hotly throughout my entire being. I hear a low sound and realize it's me, moaning his name.

"Max. Max. Come here," I say, after the waves calm and I can actually form words.

He takes his time, as usual, licking more gently now. He kisses my clit, causing another deep ripple of bliss. Then he kisses his way up my body, laying himself over me. He kisses my mouth.

I can taste *myself* and it's strange. The most wildly intimate thing imaginable. I weave my fingers through his hair. I need him. I need to grab onto him and hold him. I'm riding some crazy rush and I need him to anchor me.

"It's all right," I hear him murmur. "I'll take care of you."

Max's hot—*enormous*—cock slides against my slippery, still-pulsing pussy and I moan. The pleasure is still there, as though the wave hasn't retreated at all but is holding there, getting ready to crash all over again.

"We can take it slow, sweetheart, if you want. I can wait if you've had enough."

"*No.*"

He laughs again, even though his eyes are so lusty and dark, he almost looks dangerous. In a good way. In exactly the kind of way I need him to be right now.

"*Max.*"

"Right here, baby. You want to feel some more?"

"Yes. Yes."

"All right, then. You're going to like this."

He's adjusting me, pushing my legs wider.

"Wrap your legs around me and hold on tight."

I do. He takes the head of his cock and uses himself to rub against my hyper-sensitive clit. "I've never done this bareback before. Not once. Not only that, but I'm way out of practice and I'm already too close. So I won't last long."

I'm not even sure what he means and I don't care.

"But we've got all night," he's murmuring. "You're the most beautiful woman I've ever seen, Peach. I love the way you feel."

He pushes his big cock against my soft, slick pussy, opening me. I'm tight but I'm so wet he slides in a little. *God, he's so freaking big. How will this work?* Max uses his thumb to rub and play my clit while his other hand grips me. He's so strong I think he might leave marks on my skin and I *want* him to. It's strange but the urge is voracious: I want him to mark me and make me his. The pleasure wave starts to build again, but this time it's even stronger. Higher. More forceful. It's edged with a pain that's not really pain but more of a lower layer of pleasure. It's full of gliding friction and deep, starry heat.

"You all right, Peach?" he murmurs against my neck.

"*Oh.*" I'm incapable of complex sentences at this point. All I know is that I want more. I *need* more.

His thick cock slides deeper. The pleasure-pain surges. His cock slides back a little before pushing even deeper, stretching me. He continues this rhythm, pulling back, then pushing deeper until the melting wave of pleasure-pain is a tsunami riding a crazy-high crest. His thumb presses against my clit and it's enough. The wave crashes. The clenching spasms pull Max's massive cock deeper. He's gripping me, sliding thickly with each grip of my body until there's a small spark of pain somewhere inside this wall of pleasure as he thrusts hard and deep, until he's fully rooted inside me. His hands are on my backside now, gripping in fistfuls, ensuring total possession. All I can feel is Max. The deep throbbing pulse as his cock surges and comes. He's groaning my name. The jets of his liquid heat find some perfect trigger, setting me off again. My inner muscles squeeze him and work him as we come together in perfect rhythm. It lasts a long time. We hold onto each other, riding the bliss.

His body lays heavily over mine, his thick bulk still deeply, wetly inside me.

My arms and legs are wrapped around him, my core rippling tightly, almost lovingly.

I don't want to move. I'll never be the same. Max Black is a part of me now. The most beautiful thing. I want to keep him close to me, inside me, just like this.

"I'm so glad I waited for you," I whisper.

11

It takes me a long time to return to myself.

I've just had the most intense experience of my life.

My little Peach is quite literally a dream come true.

We're sweaty and wrapped around each other. I'm on top of her, still fully inside her. I don't want to crush her, but I also have no intention of disengaging. I carefully adjust us, so her leg is hitched around my waist. Instead of pulling out, I slide deeper. My cock is already hard again, huge and rearing and out of control. I can't quite tell if I'm still gushing from the most earth-shattering orgasm I've ever had, or spilling pre-cum from the next one. I don't really give a fuck about the differential.

I grasp her outrageously-nubile body as I kiss her. Now I know why I avoided kissing. It *is* intimate. Wildly so. I never wanted intimacy of this kind until now. With Peach, I want to get *more* than intimate. I want to feel her and eat her alive and possess her so fully she knows she's mine and *only* mine. I want everything.

She's so soft against my hardness, so feminine in my arms. I need to be careful with her. It would be so easy to hurt her.

She writhes to get closer.

Fuck. I'm going to come if she keeps doing that. I'm so close. Again.

I want more. The need to pump her full of my hot seed has become my brand new obsession. Which is fucking crazy, but there it is.

She's still kissing me, and I play her tongue with my own.

She makes a little noise of pleasure, which almost sets me off.

My hand eases over the curve of her hip. I grip her. I slide my cock out a fraction, then ease deeper.

Goddamn it. I can't hold on to this.

I'm riding a rising tide. I force myself to calm down. With every ounce of willpower I possess, I hold myself still. She's sore. I need to be careful. But then she presses against me, setting a tentative rhythm. So I slide my tongue deeper as I fuck her as sweetly as I'm capable of. Which, as it turns out, is pretty goddamn sweet.

She sighs and goes pliant against me.

"*Max*," she coos. "It's happening again. You feel too good."

I hug her closer, gripping harder and driving deeper. "Let go, baby. Let me in. That's my girl."

She's on the edge, just like I am. *God, I just can't get close enough.* She moans and I can feel her pussy squeezing and pulsing around my cock as she comes. My release explodes out of me in hot, seedy bursts. Our mouths are hungry, tasting and licking as the waves of our pleasure swell and roll. We just keep on coming.

Her hands are weaved into my hair and we're staring into each other's eyes. Hers are as blue as the summer sky. *I love you*, I want to say, but it's too soon. I don't want to scare her. I want to keep her. She's mine. I belong to her now, and all I can hope for is that I'm good enough.

IN THE MORNING I run the shower and place a couple of thick towels on the cedar bench that runs the length of the Italian sandstone shower in my master bathroom. My shower is basically as big as a car wash and has seven different jets in it. I turn on the steam and let it run for a while. I think about the little white lie I told Peach about not getting my cuff wet, in a last attempt to save myself from falling too hard, which was futile. It's actually waterproof. I go back to the bed where Peach is still curled up, asleep. Gently, I turn her to me and smooth her hair back from her face. I love her hair, with its fiery copper reds that fade to an almost white-blond at their ringlet tips.

And her angel's face. And her candy-pink lips. I kiss her softly, possessively, and she makes a little noise of protest. She wants to keep sleeping. But I gently pick her up and carry her to the shower, which is now a white-out of steam. I lay her on the bench.

"Max?" she says sleepily.

"This is your own personal spa," I tell her. "But better. Turn over. I'm going to give you the best massage you've ever had."

She pauses, but then she turns and lays on her stomach. "I've never had a massage."

"Well, then, you're in for a treat." I grab some lavender-scented oil and pour a bunch of it onto my hands. Then I start rubbing it onto her back, working the muscles in long, careful strokes.

"*Oh*. That feels so good."

"You're too young to work so hard. You take care of your staff. Your customers. Your grandmother. It's time someone took care of you."

She moans again as I find a knot of tension and work the deep tissue.

"I'm going to take care of you," I tell her, pressing harder, "and you're going to let me."

She exhales a laugh but I work another knot and she moans again. Her body is so beautifully proportioned, toned and curved and exquisite. I run my hands along her smooth skin, marveling at every detail. I had no idea a person could be *this* perfect. There's something mesmerizing and mouth-watering about the sheer magnitude of Peach's beauty, like she was designed just for me, for everything I never thought to wish for.

"This morning," I tell her, "I'm going to massage you and make you feel good. Then I'm taking you out to lunch. Later, we'll sit in the hot tub and watch the sunset."

"That sounds like a perfect day."

My fingers glide from her lower back, over her sweet little ass, roving intimately. I massage her thighs, dipping between them to rub her soft pussy. She moans again, giving me everything I want. I carefully ease her onto her back, opening her legs. I kiss and lick her pussy for a while, but I don't let her come yet. I massage her arms, her hands, her breasts, her stomach, gently. Then my fingers slide lower. I rub her clit, playing her softly, easing my fingers inside her tightness, curling them to find a sensitive spot as I tenderly squeeze and press her clit until she starts to quiver and clench in a soft, undulating rhythm. I work the rhythm of her body, spinning it out until she's supple and still-rippling. I lay over her, sliding the head of my gargantuan hard-on inside her, laying myself over her, slowly, since she's still so new at this, but forcefully. I work her orgasm further, harder, until the waves of her next climax tug tightly around my cock and I fill her in hot bursts that make her come again. I thrust deep, working the ebb of her pleasure all the way to the end. When I finally pull out, she whimpers softly. I turn on the rain shower head and the detachable, European-style jet. I wash her hair and her body, rinsing the soapy suds away. Then I use the soft jet to bring her to another rise, kissing her pussy as she comes again. She's limp and so delicious I have to kiss her again as I dry her hair and her skin. Then I carry her back to bed.

"What's my name?" she laughs dreamily.

"Dixie May Rafferty Sutton," I say softly. I love her name. I take her in my arms and hold her. I'm still adjusting to the newness of all this. The feeling of being deeply, fully slayed by her closeness.

She smiles, but her eyes close. "What's *your* name?"

"Maximillian Black," I murmur in her ear, kissing her hair.

"I think I like you a whole lot, Maximillian Black."

"I think I like you a whole lot, too, Peach pie."

"I wish I could stay here with you forever, Max. Just like this." Her words are almost slurred with comfort and satisfaction and this makes me happier than I've ever been.

She drifts into a spent, peaceful sleep and I continue to lightly kiss her pink lips and smooth her silky hair and just watch her, dazzled, fascinated and so in love I don't recognize myself. "Then why don't you?" I whisper.

12

I WAKE up in Max's arms, with his big, warm body wrapped around mine.

It all comes back to me. I remember the massage he gave me this morning. It was the kind of thing that changes your life. That ruins you for anything or anyone else. I start counting all the orgasms he gave me. Three. No, four. *Five?*

Max Black is a magician. He is so very good at… *making me come.* And making me feel safe. It's a little disconcerting how attached I've become, to him and the way he makes me feel.

The sweep of my eyelashes against his corded neck wakes him. He smiles gently at me. He's so handsome it literally takes my breath away. But then his expression changes. "Wow."

"Wow?"

"I'm still here," he murmurs sleepily.

"Where else would you be?"

"I usually wake up. But I didn't have any dreams last night," he says. "At all. It's the first time in a very long time that I haven't been woken up by nightmares."

I probably should have considered that, after what happened earlier. But I didn't. Weirdly, it didn't even cross my mind. "You still get them a lot?"

"Every night."

"Every night?"

"Yes. Until you. See? You have fixed me."

"I'm sure it's not that easy."

"Maybe it is. Maybe I just needed a sassy little Southern belle in my bed to shoo away all my demons."

"Sassy?"

He squeezes my ass and I squirm. "Sassy and cute and sexy and beautiful." He smiles mischievously. "And *very* responsive to a certain thing I do with my tongue."

My face gets hot and he smiles.

"Which I plan to do again at my very first opportunity. But first I want to take you out to lunch."

I try to ignore a wave of unease. If we go out to lunch it means we have to…go out.

Where *he* might be waiting.

Max seems to read my anxiety. "I'll be right there with you. There's nothing to worry about. I'm going to take you to a rooftop French bistro I go to sometimes. It's only two blocks away."

I *am* hungry. And Max is right. I can't hide. In two days I have to go back to work.

He climbs out of bed and I watch him as he pulls on his jeans. He's so freaking buff. So big and impressively built. So *hard*. I have no basis for comparison but some attuned female instinct can sense that Max Black is extraordinary. In every possible way. He has a *beautiful* body. Which is probably a strange way to describe it, but the only one that does it justice. His cock is…not quite what I imagined. It's far bigger. Harder. Silky. *I wonder if he'd let me taste him. Lick him. Suck on him…like he did to me.*

But he tucks himself into his jeans, with effort. He pulls on a shirt. Then he takes a revolver out of his bedside table drawer. He checks something on it, then he slides it into the back of his jeans, so it's sticking out of his waistband.

"Max?"

"Yeah?"

"You have a *gun*?"

"Yes." Like it's no big deal.

"You can't take that to *lunch*."

"I'll keep it hidden. No one will know."

"But—"

"Peach," he says softly, "*Your* psycho stalker has already assaulted you once and then attempted to do it again. *I'm* being framed for a felony I didn't commit, most likely by a crazy bitch who clearly has no limits. Being prepared is our best option." Without a single reservation about this whole thing, apparently, he peels the duvet off me. "Come on. Get up." He sees…*all* of me, and blinks. Then he shakes his head a little. "I don't think I could ever get used to that."

"Get used to what?"

"You. And how fucking gorgeous you are. Now get dressed. Before I fall to my knees and start ravaging you all over again."

I blush—*damn it*—and pull on one of the dresses Max bought for me.

"I need to buy you more clothes," he says. "Maybe we could go shopping after lunch."

"I'd rather come back here and watch the sunset with you in the hot tub."

He pulls on a jacket, which hides his gun. "You're right. I'll just call them and order more, now that I know your size."

We take the elevator down and walk out onto the street. It's a sunny fall Sunday afternoon in L.A. It feels strange to be back in reality again, with people going about their business like it's any other day. Like life hasn't just been transformed into a fairy tale of hot sex and shower massages and revelations that have the power to touch the very depths of your body and soul.

Max takes my hand. I look up at him and he winks at me. "Okay?" he says.

"Okay." Because he's with me, I *am* okay. Without him, I'm not sure I would be. I don't bother analyzing this. Is it a problem that Max now feels necessary? Possibly. Should I be worried that, when I leave or when we both resume our regular lives, the thought of being apart from him makes me feel like I'll shatter into a million tiny pieces? Probably. But with his hand firmly grasping mine, I put it out of my mind. We're together. We have the whole day to spend together, and tomorrow. Then he might do some work from the restaurant.

I can't think beyond that. I'm surprised to find that it *hurts* to even consider a day or even an hour without him near me.

This is not good.

It's impossible not to notice the looks Max gets as we walk past several women. One even stops walking and watches him as we walk past.

I understand why they would stare.

He's mine, is what I'm thinking. *Mine.*

Peach. Chill. But I can't.

We get to the bistro and it's got a view of the skyline and is decorated with hanging lanterns and leafy plants in big pots. Soft music plays. "This is nice, Max. This is the first time I've been out to eat since I opened the restaurant."

"You work too much," he says.

The hostess shows us to our table. She ogles Max and offers to take his jacket but he keeps it on.

We don't talk about it but I think we're both relieved. No one followed us.

Max orders a bottle of champagne and we clink glasses and this whole thing feels magical. Surreal. Almost too good to be true. He takes my hand across the table. "Don't be mad at me."

"Why would I be?"

"Because I'm about to say something that's going to make me sound like a lunatic."

"I already know you're a lunatic."

He's not expecting this. He smiles and makes a face. Then he gives me a look I'll never forget. "When I tell you what I'm about to tell you, I want you to just absorb it and not feel like you need to reply to it."

I have no idea what he means. "All right."

Max can see that he's got me curious. He sits back in his chair and folds his arms, knees apart, all god-like gorgeousness and alpha male charisma. "Actually, I don't think you're ready."

He's teasing me now. I glare at him.

He laughs. *God, I love the sound of his laughter and the little crinkle at the edge of his blue eyes when he smiles.*

"So you're not going to tell me?"

"Oh, I'm going to tell you. I just need to be able to kiss you immediately afterwards, so I've decided to wait."

I wouldn't have immediately picked him for a romantic, but the more I get to know him—which is in fact pretty well at this point—the more I'm learning that Max isn't just a good person, he's sensitive and kind and, well, an absolute sweetheart. All that, when you combine it with the total package is sort of mind-blowing.

Can something that seems too good to be true…actually be *too good to be true?*

And I have a feeling I know what he's going to tell me. Later. When he can kiss me immediately afterwards. And I can kiss him.

I smile, playing his game, but somewhere deep inside my heart, I feel panicky. Because I feel the same way.

My phone rings. I pull it out of my bag. Grandma Bea.

"Do you mind if I take this, Max? I talk to my grand-mother every Sunday afternoon. It's sort of our thing. I'll make it quick."

"Go right ahead. I'll order for us."

I answer the phone and talk to Grandma Bea for a few minutes. "The roof is leaking again," she says. "The young man who put a board over the hole for us was *such* a darlin' and all the girls set out their lawn chairs to watch him work."

"I'll send someone to do it properly," I tell her. I can't afford a new roof for the whole house yet, which it desperately needs, but I can at least afford to do more than have a board nailed over a hole. And it reminds me of my grand plans, to earn enough money to pay Grandma Bea back and to fix up her house for her. Will I still be able to?

"Don't you worry your pretty little head over it, sweetie," says Grandma Bea. "The girls and I have hired Jackson to weed the garden, too."

Max tops up our drinks.

I talk to Grandma Bea a while longer, then end the call.

"What'd you say the name of your home town in Georgia is?" he says.

"We're just outside of Savannah."

"And Grandma Bea is your mother's mother?"

"Yes."

"So that would make her…Bea Rafferty?"

I'm not sure why he's asking all these questions. "Yes."

Our food arrives. It's real French food, steak with butter melted over the top with roasted potatoes and vegetables. It's delicious. Max and I talk about a new business he's just started building. It's an app, he says, for investors who don't know a lot about investing.

"It works like a game. You can play it on your phone. The better you get at the game, the more sophisticated the trading gets."

"That's a great idea, Max. I've always wanted to invest in the stock market but I never learned how. It seems so complicated."

"I think a lot of people feel the same way. It's actually not complicated at all, if you know what to look for. That's what this app will help people do. It'll help you choose your investments based on easy-to-learn, real-time data."

"So this is what you do with your time off," I tease him. "You're worse than me."

We finish our meals and after a while, Max asks, "So, do you have a quiet little corner table at Peach's where I can set up my office?"

"If you're sure you want to do that—"

"I am."

"I think I can find something."

THE TIME I've spent with Max feels charmed and sacred, sparked with hope. But there's more to it than that. We're shielded for now, by our little weekend window. We can dedicate our time to each other without the distractions of work or other people. Or the very real threats to each of us that promise to break our bubble and possibly destroy it altogether.

Our time feels finite. It feels like it has to end. Nothing's this good. Nothing ever has been. It can't last.

Will I be able to handle being followed and threatened with violence for much longer? Will the stalker find me? Could he follow me back to Georgia? Yes, because he knows who I am and probably knows my name and it's not that hard to track people down these days. Will I have to go somewhere else, to hide? Will he hurt me? Will he hurt my family? Will he kill me?

Max, too, even though he's got a good lead, still isn't entirely sure who framed him. *Will she do it again? Will she plague him for years to come? Will he end up in jail because she couldn't have him and now she wants revenge?*

Because of all these questions, which we don't talk about but which hang over our heads like invisible guillotines, we're even more intense about this *thing* that's happening between us.

We hold hands all the way back from the restaurant. There's no more talk of going shopping or anything else. We both want to get back to Max's. We've held back for more than an hour. As the elevator door shuts us back into our haven, Max leads me straight to his bedroom.

He sits down on his bed. He pulls me between his knees, so I'm standing close to him. I take his face in my hands and I kiss him slowly.

"I'll protect you with my life," he whispers.

I don't want him to say that. I can't bear it, the thought of anything happening to him. *I'll* kill the stalker myself before I let anything happen to Max.

How dare he threaten me? Even worse, how dare he threaten us?

Max takes his gun and sets it on his bedside table. Then he eases me back and rolls us over so I'm on top of him. I kiss him. This is all happening so fast...because we *want* it to happen fast. There's nothing to doubt with him. Since I'm spending the weekend in bed with Max Black, there's no point holding back. I want to *feel*, as much as I can. Because he feels so damn good. "There's something

I've been thinking about," I murmur, touching the top button of his shirt.

"What's that?"

I unbutton his button and let my fingers slide to the next one. "It's not really fair."

"What's not fair?"

"That you… " It's a hard thing to explain.

"That I… ?"

I touch the waistband of his jeans, unfastening his button. "I want to kiss you…like you kiss me."

His gaze gets hot. "Maybe we should wait until you're a little more used to all this."

"I don't want to wait."

Slowly, I lower his zipper. I start to push his jeans lower on his hips. He helps me. His cock springs free and it's huge and hard. He must be the most perfectly-made man in the world. Or maybe he's just perfect for me. Tentatively at first, I ease my fingers around him.

"*Fuck*," he exhales. "I don't—"

"Shh." I kiss a line down his chest. His stomach. I lick the head of his cock, where a bead of moisture has gathered. He's salty and enticing, so incredibly *male*.

I take more of him and Max groans. I lick him and suck on him lovingly, until he comes in my mouth in thick bursts. He's mine. I want all of him. I *drink* him, as much as I can, but it's too much. It spill downs my chin.

Max pulls me up and holds me in his arms. He uses the sheet to wipe my face. Then he places his finger over my lips. His blue eyes are bloodshot and the look he gives me melts my heart into something that belongs wholly to him and only him.

So *this* is what it feels like to want something so badly you don't care if it breaks your heart, because you know it's absolutely worth it.

I WAKE with my throbbing beast of a cock wedged between her legs. My body is spooned around her. In my sleep, I've enveloped her body with mine. She seems to have replaced my nightmares with fantasies. She's so much smaller than I am, so soft and sexy. I kiss her neck and she coos, half-asleep, half-lust-drowsed. Her legs open a little. Her back arches and her sweetness cradles my raging cock.

I adjust her body as I want, as gently as I'm capable of, easing her onto her stomach as I bite and lick my way down her body, lifting her hips and spreading her knees. My tongue burrows and she squirms but I hold her down and lick her everywhere I want, thrusting my tongue into her. My fingers play and squeeze and rub her clit as I taste her with my greedy tongue. She's moaning my name and her pussy starts to tighten, so I climb up her body, gently pushing her head down and keeping her hips high. I press my engorged cock to her slippery entrance. I know she's sore and I'm pushing her hard but I can't help it. My lust has never been so voracious. The more I have of her, the more I want. "I need you so much, baby. Will you take me like this?" I growl darkly, wondering if I'll be able to stop myself if she refuses.

"*Yes*," she breathes and I slide my thick, spilling cock deep into all that tight, juicy wetness. I'm almost coming already. I'm fighting to hold on.

When she cries out I start to lose it. I keep myself still, letting her body adjust to my forceful invasion. My addiction is a monster that wants to go harder and deeper, to fill her up with my hot cum. I go slow, twisting her hair around my fist as I thrust in and out of her, stroking her squeezing pussy with my pulsing cock. She arches back against me and I give her more. I give her everything she can take. She moans and starts coming hard. Her inner muscles clamp tightly around me, massaging the length of me in firm tugs until I lose all control. My release rages out of me in throbbing jets, flooding her until it's dripping down her thighs.

She's limp with sated pleasure and I wrap her in my body, spooning her, adoring her, keeping my still-hard cock deep inside all that sweet, wet perfection. My hands grip her and touch her possessively. I play her nipples and her clit, memorizing every perfect curve and groove, until she's coming again. I taste her skin and drink in her scent, of peaches and moonlight and sex. I want to do this all day and all night, forever. I want to live like this, coming inside her, kissing her and holding her close to my beating, breaking heart.

"I love you, Peach. I love you." Then I kiss her again.

I'M SO WEIRDLY CONTENT, it takes me a minute to realize something's going on. A noise. Pounding.

Boom boom boom.

What the fuck. Is it my heart? My head?

It's the door. Someone's knocking.

There's only one person in the world who's *that* obnoxious.

My brother.

I consider not even answering the door. But it's Rafe: I always answer the door. It's our pact. If I don't answer he'll think I'm dead, or worse. He'll end up breaking in or something equally stupid. Not only that, but somewhere through the haze of my lust, I know I'm probably going to need his help. His relationship with the law is a lot more secure than mine. And if I'm going to keep Peach safe, I at least need to attempt to do it legally. Otherwise I'm pretty sure I'll end up in a goddamn prison cell.

Which can't happen. Because I can't be near her if I'm locked up.

I need to be as close to her as possible. I need to keep her with me at all times.

She's become the only reason I want to keep breathing.

"Who's here?" she says.

"My brother and his wife must be back from their honeymoon."

Boom boom boom.

"I should probably let them in before he breaks down the door," I say, but I can't bring myself to let go of her.

I kiss her again.

She giggles and it's the cutest, sweetest sound. Her smile feels like moonlight, like a shot of pure, pure ecstasy.

"I don't want to answer it," I tell her. "I want to stay here with you."

Boom boom boom. "Max. Open the door. I know you're in there."

"Sounds like they really want to talk to you," she says.

To the door, I yell, "Hold on a fucking second."

I pull away from her, already feeling bereft. I do my best to clean us up. Her dress is bunched up on the floor, ripped. I bought her three, and the two others are out by the hot tub, possibly. I grab one of my t-shirts out of my closet. She holds it up. It's miles too big and hangs down to the middle of her thighs. "Stanford?"

"I got my MBA there. I'll buy you some more clothes. Until then, you'll just have to wear this."

She puts my t-shirt on and just seeing her in it makes me feel ludicrously happy. Now if I can just convince her to move in with me, marry me, have my babies and grow old with me…

But all that will have to wait. There is one thing I can do now, though, so I do. I can't help it: I kiss her again. I feel like I have a knack for this kissing thing, when it comes to Peach.

Boom boom boom.

"Jesus Christ," I mutter, zipping up my jeans and grabbing a clean shirt which I pull over my head.

I walk out to the door and let Rafe and Lexi in.

They look glamorous and sun-tanned, and different, somehow. Like a few weeks of deep immersion into uninterrupted bliss has tempered them into the best possible versions of themselves. My brother, understandably, has spent most of his life working like a maniac. He's driven and relentless in his pursuit of money and power, to such an extent that he's probably made a lot more enemies than friends over the years. Partly because he doesn't have time for being nice. All that started to change when he met Lexi, though. He fell so hard for her I think he would've let his empire crumble around him just to keep her. I now understand what that feels like.

Rafe slaps me on the back and Lexi hugs me. She smells like flowers and sunshine. Her blond hair is a shade lighter than it was before they left, and her green eyes spangle.

"Italy agreed with you two." I'm glad to see them, despite the interruption. They're the only people in the world I actually choose to spend time with. Aside from my new little Georgia girl who I plan on following around like an adoring puppy until the day I die.

Which might turn out to be sooner than I'd hoped.

14

I'VE MET Max's brother and his new sister-in-law once before, under very different circumstances.

I feel flushed. And enlightened. My entire body is buzzing and the world has taken on a glittering tint. Like I'm seeing it with new, star-struck eyes.

Wow. All that was…outrageously intimate.

Despite the obviousness of the situation—me wearing Max's shirt and both of us looking dazed and mussed-up —I stand in the doorway of his bedroom. I watch Max with his family and I can't help marveling at the sight of him. His thick, glorious hair is unruly from my fingers. The t-shirt he's wearing is worn and clings to the sculpted muscles of his brawny shoulders and chest, revealing the ink on his tanned arms. Stubble darkens his handsome face. He looks big, tousled, a little bit dangerous. And utterly delicious.

Which he is. He loved what I did to him. He came so hard. So much. His essence is inside me. I'm changed by him. I feel him.

They don't see me at first.

"Have you eaten?" his brother says, unpacking a shopping bag full of food. He looks a lot like Max—tall and dark and gorgeous—but his hair is black instead of dark brown. And he's not as perfectly…*Max* as Max. "We brought dinner."

Rafe looks up when Max doesn't answer—he's smiling at me. Rafe does a double-take when he sees me standing in the doorway. His jaw actually drops.

I blush. I'm wearing Max's shirt. My hair is wild. I'm sure it's very obvious that we just rolled out of a very intense session in bed.

Max doesn't seem to mind. He walks over to me and slides his arm around me. He leads me to the marble kitchen island. "Peach, I'd like you to meet my brother Rafe and his wife, Lexi. You met them once before, at the restaurant. Remember?"

"Hi," I say, blushing even more when Max kisses my cheek. "Of course I remember."

"Peach is going to be staying with me for a while," Max says. His arm tightens around my waist and he's looking at me with this crazy expression on his face, of such tenderness it almost brings tears to my eyes.

Lexi and Rafe glance at each other, then at Max, then at me, like they're having trouble processing all this. Maybe Max hasn't had a guest in a while. Maybe a long while. They clearly weren't expecting me, or anyone else, to be here with him.

Max smiles. "My brother is speechless so rarely I must say I'm enjoying this."

Rafe seems to regain some of his composure. He looks at his brother. Then he walks over and gives me a kiss on the cheek. "Peach, it's very nice to meet you. I'm glad you're here. He's been talking about you non-stop since that night we ate at your restaurant."

I look at Max and he shrugs. "The pie."

Lexi gives me a little hug. "So nice to meet you, Peach."

"You too, Lexi. Nice to meet you both."

Her eyes are a bright shade of sea-green. Something about her makes me think she's seen her own share of hardships. There's an undercurrent of vulnerability about her. She's probably around my age, maybe even a little younger. She's gorgeous in an off-hand kind of way, like she has no idea how beautiful she is. "How's the restaurant going?"

"Great. We just keep getting busier and busier."

"I can see why," she says. "Your food is amazing."

"Thank you. I'm looking into renting the place across the street, as a bakery. The pies have become a much bigger part of the business than I expected. It sort of makes sense to separate the two."

"That's so fantastic."

"I still have to put the deposit down for the new place

and hire a few more staff, so I'm not completely sure it'll go ahead yet."

That is, if I don't get assaulted again first, or worse.

"You should definitely go for it," she says. "I know it'll be a huge success. I've seen the write-ups you've been getting."

Max grabs a bottle of red wine from a rack and starts opening it. "I'm going to be working from Peach's for a while. Someone's been following her. I've hired a few bodyguards but—"

"What do you mean, following her?" Rafe says.

"Peach has…a stalker." Max seems to have trouble saying the word. "She's been assaulted once and he showed up again a few nights ago."

"*Shit,*" Rafe says.

Lexi gasps. "Oh my gosh."

"Luckily, Max was there. He saved me." The way I've said it sounds melodramatic, but it's true. He did save me.

"The cops have been patrolling the area," Max says darkly. "Peach has a beeper, and a restraining order is in place. Which means nothing, of course. I'm going to base myself at the restaurant and work from there."

Rafe is watching his brother, like he's surprised by how intense Max is being. A stalker is something to be intense about, sure, but Max's whole manner has become almost manic.

"I have a couple of guys I use," Rafe says. "They're thorough. And discrete."

"Good. We can add them to the guards I've already got in place, then."

I didn't actually realize Max had hired people. Bodyguards, of all things.

They talk logistics and it makes me feel uneasy. It reminds me of how terrified I am. I'm glad when Rafe changes the subject. "And what's all this about a woman named Melanie being the one who framed you?" Rafe asks Max. "Are you sure?"

Max sighs, like he wishes we didn't have to talk about this. "No. But it's… " He runs a hand through his hair. " …probably her."

"Who is she?"

"A mistake."

"Did you date her?" Rafe clearly has no problem spearing to the heart of the matter.

Max is uncomfortable with the whole topic. "No, I didn't *date* her. I met her at a charity event around seven months ago. She said she worked for a tech company. As a coder or something. I spent a few hours with her. She's been showing up at work and writing to me ever since."

"Writing to you?"

"Yes."

"What, like love letters?"

Max is exasperated. "More like harassment letters. I shred them."

"Did you—?" Rafe catches himself. He doesn't have

to finish his question. We all know what he was going to say…*sleep with her?*

Max is pissed off. "She made me feel lonelier than I ever had. And that's saying something." *So I guess that's a yes.* He's watching me. There's a desperation to him that I can't quite read. I get the feeling it's important to him that I believe him.

"Okay," Rafe says, noticing the fever and emotion behind Max's delivery. "But why is she hacking your email and framing you? And how the fuck did she get a hold of your laptop in the first place? Did she do it here in your home office, or at your main office? Or somewhere else?"

"She never came here." He glances over at the glassed-in corner area by the window, where there's a desk with stacks of paper on it. Max is holding his hair in one of his fists, like he did…after he put his hands on my neck. I want to unclench it. To tell him everything will be okay. I know Max well enough by now to understand that none of this is his fault. So he slept with some random woman he met at a charity event, six or seven months before he met me. I can hardly blame him for that. Or her. "She didn't need the laptop. She could have hacked my email account from anywhere. The next time I opened the email account, I would have uploaded whatever virus or encrypted software she planted—but we can't figure out how the hell she did it."

The way Max says it sounds defeated, which fires me

up. It's not okay. I can understand why this woman wanted Max and won't give up trying to convince him to be with her. But to use all that to get him *arrested?* Who does that? He doesn't deserve this. I put my hand around his fist, gently, where he's holding his hair. I open his fingers, one by one. Then I lower his hand so it's resting on his thigh.

Rafe watches me do this for a few seconds.

Lexi pours four glasses of wine, and slides one to each of us.

"So let me get this straight," Rafe says. "You spent one night with Melanie seven months ago. She came to your office and continues sending letters. When you told her you weren't interested, she hacked into your email account and framed you for insider trading."

"That pretty much sums it up."

"Wow." Rafe takes a sip of his wine. "But how would she have gotten a hold of your password?"

"If I knew that, brother, I wouldn't be wearing this cuff. I guess that's what hackers do: bypass shit like that. Mike is looking into it, but whatever she uploaded, it's all encrypted. He can't find which email it came in through. It's beyond the scope of what he knows how to do."

"Mike's one of the best we have," Rafe says. "We'll have to find someone who's a next level expert."

"I know someone who might be able to help," I offer. "He's a good friend of my bartender. His name is Charlie

Shaw. He owns…" I try to recall the name of Charlie's company. "I think it's called Blue Sky Tech Solutions."

"I've heard of them." Rafe sounds impressed. It's the same vibe I've seen every time Johnny or someone else mentions Charlie's company. You get the feeling Charlie is very, very good at whatever he does.

"I can get his number." I'm pretty sure Charlie will make it a priority. It's Max, after all, and I've already noticed that people go out of their way for him. Max has an aura to him. Dark, glittery alpha stardust clings to him. People stare at him. They *want* him. Sometimes so much that when they can't have him, they handle it badly, apparently. "I'll try to get you a meeting with him tomorrow morning."

Max nods, but he's gone quiet. The shadows under his eyes are darker. He looks big and mean. All his damages seem more pronounced. Some flare-up of remembered pain clings to him.

"We'll get what we need, Max," says Rafe. "Don't worry."

But something in Max has shifted. My tender lover has been overtaken by the old demons that haunt him, and by new ones, too, this is easy to see. Now that I know where some of them stem from, I feel deeply affected by this, as though his pain has lodged itself right in the middle of my heart. It's a strange feeling. An irrevocable bond has forged between us. Strangely, it makes me feel stronger than I ever have.

How dare you, Melanie, whoever you are, is what I'm thinking. *He's good, he's mine, and I'm not going to let you hurt him like this.* "Everything will be okay, Max, you'll see."

Either that, or it won't be.

MAX SHUTS the door behind Rafe and Lexi.

"*Fuck*," he exhales.

He seems agitated and surly.

"Do you want to be alone for a while, Max? It's fine if you do. I can—"

"No." He's standing behind me. His voice is deep and quiet. He's looming there so close to me in the low-lit room. His warm fingers graze the hem of my long shirt.

Max turns me and eases me against the wall, so I can feel the hard ridge of him against my stomach.

"What even *is* insider trading?"

His fingers slide higher and his thigh forces my legs further apart. "If I were to tell you that a company called Beatty-Williamson is going to be taken over next week by a larger company, called Heathman-Cole Securities…" Max tugs my panties aside and I gasp. He's so big. He seems like he's walking some fine line tonight, between the Max I know and something else. Something danger-ous. I go shamelessly wet as his thumb skates tenderly over my clit. His fingers slide inside me, his knuckles finding some insanely sensitive trigger. "This is information the public doesn't know, so if I told you to buy shares now because their value will skyrocket after the takeover, and you do…" He unzips his jeans, releasing himself. "Can you handle it?" he whispers.

I'm sore, and no wonder. But I don't care. I know his darkest secrets. I've seen his fury and I've felt his pain. My hunger for him has been lit at the basest, most urgent level. Something in me has become feral and ravenous, as though there's nothing I wouldn't do. I *need* him, like I've never needed anything in my life. "Can *you* handle it?" I whisper back.

"No," he says. "I can't handle anything about you, baby. You're killing me. I can't get enough."

"Then I guess you better keep going."

Max lifts me. His massive cock presses against my soft, humid flesh and the hyper-sensitive nub. The wash of pleasure is crazily intense. Maddening. " …and then," he continues, "if you sell those shares at a huge profit the week after that…that would be insider trading."

"Is that *true*?" I breathe. "Is that—*oh*—actually going to happen?"

"Yes."

"Don't tell me that."

"Why not? Are you going to run out and buy some shares?"

His cock thrusts into me, hotly, thickly. It hurts but I

can already feel the rushes starting, quivering around his huge bulk. He drives deeper. He's rough but in a way that's so controlled, so totally *aware* of me. He continues his upward plunges, again and again, until the pleasure tips over and I come hard, clenching around him in soft, succulent pulls. I feel Max shudder as his own release pumps into me in thick, rhythmic throbs.

It's a while before either of us moves. I feel dazed, lust-drunk and so in love with him it's disorienting. Like falling off a cliff when you didn't even realize you were close to the edge.

"I won't tell anyone," I whisper.

"I know." Max pulls out wetly, then he lifts me carefully into his arms. He carries me to his bed. He tucks me in. He sits next to me, watching my face, fingering the end strands of my hair.

"Aren't you coming to bed?"

"I have some work stuff to finish up."

"It's after midnight."

"I'm a night owl."

He seems distracted. "Are you okay, Max?'

He smiles but it doesn't reach his eyes.

Max leaves me to sleep. I think about going to him but decide that maybe he wants some space. I'm tired and eventually I sleep.

But I miss him.

※

WHEN I WAKE UP, Max isn't in bed. I get up and walk out of his bedroom to find Max sitting at the dining table, working on his laptop. He's clean-shaven. His hair is still wet from his shower. Playing off his clean-cut look is the blinking criminal's cuff, the inked edge of a tattoo on his neck, where his collar is open, the shadows under his eyes. It's so *Max*, I'm learning: his darkness and his light, constantly at war. It's one of the things I've come to love most about him.

"Hi," I say, shy despite myself.

He smiles. "Hi."

"You didn't come to bed."

"I…uh, slept on the couch last night."

I know why. The nightmares. They were close to the surface last night.

I wish I could rip them out of him. I wish I could fix him.

He dodges the issue. "I decided to have breakfast delivered." The counter, I notice it then, is covered in platters of fruit, bread, cheese and all kinds of other delicacies. Chilled bottles of orange juice and champagne sit on ice, and there's a freshly-brewed pot of coffee. "I've had a few more things delivered."

This time it's not just shopping bags but *racks*. And stacked boxes labelled with names like Balenciaga, Jimmy Choo, Chanel. "Max. You didn't have to—"

"There's one other thing." He looks down at a small box sitting next to his computer.

"What is it?"

"Just a little something for you."

"Max. You don't need to give me gifts."

His slow smile is doing strange things to me. Touching on all those base urges he lit last night. "Come here."

I walk over to him and he opens the box so I can see what's inside. It's a delicate platinum cuff with embedded rubies. It's like his.

"For stealing my heart." He laughs. "Sorry. That was so cheesy. But it's true."

I let him put the bracelet on my wrist. "We match," I say.

"Yeah, we match." He stands, and kisses me lightly on the mouth. Then he gets me a cup of coffee.

I shower, eat some breakfast and pick out one of the couture dresses. A black Ralph Lauren shift dress with suede detailing and a cute pearl-and-leather belt. I pull on some black Chanel ankle boots. A perfect fit.

At ten o'clock, Rafe arrives, and soon after, Charlie— and Johnny, who couldn't resist.

After the introductions are made and coffee has been served, we all sit on the couches in Max's palatial living room. Max grabs his laptop. He's wearing worn Levi's (and filling them out like nobody's business) and a nice shirt with the sleeves rolled up.

Charlie plugs a small, high-tech-looking device into the USB port.

"You don't need my password?" Max asks.

"No." Charlie smiles, like it's a funny question. He looks through Max's computer files and his email account. "This computer is completely infected. Everything's been touched."

"After I found out, I bought a new laptop and started a new email account," Max says grimly.

"Good idea." Charlie shows us the screen. "Here's the email it came in through. Dated September 2. It's in your trash."

Max looks at it. "It had a similar email address to one of my brokers. But there was no message. I tried to delete it but it wouldn't delete."

"It has what we call an anchor attached to it. Whoever this woman is, she's good. This is a sophisticated set-up. This anchor gives her access to everything on this computer. Do you have any sensitive material on here?"

"*Everything* on there was sensitive. I've deleted a lot. Or printed it, then re-entered it onto my new computer."

"You haven't transferred files from one computer to the other? Every file will be infected."

"No," Max confirms. "I suspected whatever virus she planted might be contagious. I've been careful."

Charlie checks both computers and he's satisfied the new one is clean. "The only problem is, I can't trace this email. It's encrypted. So we can't prove it was her."

"Which means," says Rafe, "that we can't clear Max's name."

"At this point, no." Charlie takes a sip of his coffee.

"But with these revenge cases, nine times out of ten the perpetrator does it again."

Max does not look comforted by this information. "If she does it again, I go directly to jail without collecting two hundred."

"Do you have some paper?" asks Charlie.

Max goes over to his desk. He comes back and places a pen and a piece of paper on the coffee table.

We all watch as Charlie writes, *It's likely this apartment has been bugged. She'll be fishing for information. Be careful.*

My investigators checked it thoroughly and didn't find anything, Max writes.

Charlie scrawls a reply. *If her bugging skills are as good as her hacking skills, they may have missed it.*

Bugged?

So, this whole time Max and I have spent together here in his apartment…she might have been listening?

Max goes into a sort of frenzy, searching through his apartment for the bug, if there even is one. He looks in drawers, running his fingers around the rims of the paintings on the walls, checking under the surfaces of the chairs and tables.

We all help him, but no one finds anything. Until Charlie finds a small stack of mail on Max's desk. He holds up a pink card. Unopened. "Max?"

Max walks over to Charlie.

"Do you get a lot of these?"

"They come a few times a week," Max says.

"What do you do with them?"

"Shred them."

Charlie opens the card. The stationery is thick pink paper. Charlie feels the corner, carefully ripping apart the seam of the paper. He holds something tiny between his fingers. Max mutters a low oath. He goes to the corner, where the shredder is sitting on the floor. He opens it, taking out handfuls of shredded paper. He reaches into the shredder, picking out one, two, three of the tiny metal bugs. When he's done, he has around ten of them in the palm of his hand.

Charlie goes to his open briefcase, which has all kinds of weird-looking devices in it, and picks out a small metal canister. He holds it up. "Soundproof."

He takes the bugs from Max and puts all of them into the canister, sealing it. "I can record these when I get back to the office so you can listen to whatever she's heard."

"That *bitch.*" Rafe looks at Max. "I just hope you haven't said anything that she could use."

Shit. He has. That stuff about those companies and the takeover.

Charlie closes his briefcase and stands up. "Can I take this computer with me, Max? I'll work on deactivating the anchor."

"Sure."

"There's no chance of tracing the email?" Rafe asks.

"No," Charlie confirms. "But if I can somehow get access to her computer for twenty minutes, I'm sure I can find all the evidence we'd need."

Rafe holds up the pink letter. "Here's her phone number."

"What are you suggesting I do?" Max says.

"Arrange to meet with her."

"No." Max is pacing.

But Rafe is undeterred. "At her office."

Charlie shakes his head. "It'll have to be at a place where we can also be there, undetected. A house, maybe. With an outdoor area. Call a truce. Say you want to discuss a business opportunity. You can offer her a glass of champagne and take a stroll through the garden. She'll leave her laptop behind and I can get what we need. From the look of this letter… " Charlie takes it from where Rafe has set it on the marble island. "…*I'll do anything just to see you once more, Max. Anything.*' …I'd say she'll agree to whatever you offer."

"The house in Malibu," Rafe suggests.

"It's out of my zone." Max sits heavily onto the couch.

"By the time they trace your whereabouts and follow you there," Charlie says, "we'll have all the evidence we need to prove you've been framed."

"And what if we don't?" Max's phone pings and he pulls it out of his pocket to look at it. "Well, she didn't waste time."

"What do you mean?" Rafe asks.

"Mike just received an email from me." Max glances at me. "Telling him to aggressively buy Beatty-Williamson shares before the takeover by Heathman-Cole Securities next week."

15

Fuck.

At this point I'll probably end up going to jail for throttling that bitch into next week before they even manage to hunt me down for the new leak. I knew Melanie was a piece of work but this is really taking it to another level. Framing me, getting me convicted of a felony, bugging my apartment and now putting the final nail in my coffin.

The thing that pisses me off the most, weirdly, isn't the felony, the hacking, the encrypted "anchor"…it's the fact that she invaded *our* privacy. She listened in on the sweetest and most life-changing events of my life to date. And it wasn't *hers* to be a part of. It's *ours*. Mine and Peach's. My Georgia girl is watching me from where she's leaning against the back of the couch in her cute little outfit with her eyes as blue as the summer sky and her hair spilling over her shoulders in coiled golden-copper waves. As stunning as she's ever been.

How dare that crazy psycho intrude on us?

I find that I want to ask her that question. I want to get the dirt on her so we can turn the tables and put an end to this shit once and for all.

"Fine." I'm still holding my phone, still reeling from the fact that the cops are probably going to be banging down my door within a matter of days or even hours and —even worse—that every word we've said this weekend may as well have been broadcast over a fucking loud-speaker.

I call the number written on the pink piece of paper Rafe's holding, dreading this.

She answers on the third ring. "Hello?"

"Hey, Melanie."

There's a pause. "Max? Is that you?"

"I'd like to meet with you. Tomorrow night."

"You…you *would?*"

There are a lot of things I want to say to Melanie right now, and none of them are remotely kind, but instead, I keep it light. It's not hard to reel her in. "I shouldn't have ignored you like that. I want to apologize to you. In person. I also have a business proposition I'd like to talk to you about. You said you're a coder, right? I was hoping maybe we could call a truce."

"Oh, Max, I'd *love* that."

"Good. How does six o'clock work for you? Can you

make it out to Malibu? I have a place by the beach out there."

"Of course. Six is perfect. I can't wait to see you. I'm going to make everything up to you, Max, you'll see. I promise you won't regret it."

Seriously? "I know I won't. Let me give you the address. Do you have a pen?"

I give Melanie the address of Rafe's house in Malibu.

"You might want to bring your portable office with you so we can go through some ideas."

"Oh. Okay." She briefly hesitates but curiosity gets the better of her. "Does this have anything to do with your app?"

Of course she knows about my app. She's been listening in on my conversations, for fuck knows how long. "Yeah, it does," I lie, then force myself to say it. "It'll be good to see you again."

"I'm sorry about everything, Max. I didn't know how else to get your attention. I've missed you so much."

Fucking hell. "See you tomorrow."

I end the call. I feel sort of sick. Melanie is literally the very last person on Earth I want to spend time with. Then again, having this out with her on the beach in Malibu will be a hell of a lot less painful than spending the next three or more years in a goddamn jail cell. Or at least mildly less painful.

"Nicely done," says Charlie. He's packing up his stuff, which includes my infected laptop. "I'll get everything ready. We should probably get there by four at the latest so we can get wires and cameras in place."

After Rafe and Charlie and Johnny leave, I stand up and walk over to Peach. I twirl a long curl of her hair around one of my fingers. "I'm sorry about all this."

"It's not your fault, Max."

She's right. Nothing's our fault. Not Melanie. Not Peach's stalker. Why do people keep inflicting their evil into our perfect little world? I find myself fantasizing about a future where we're free. Where no one bothers us. Just me and her and all the things I want to give her. With no intruders. No obsessed freaks trying to get a piece of us. I'm going to make that happen. I'm going do whatever it takes to get us to a peaceful place where I can lavish her with gifts and lust and money and a life that's all about making her happy.

I hope I can.

She takes my hand and pulls me toward the bedroom. As gorgeous and perfect as she is, I feel fucking exhausted. Dark and dirty, from faking niceties with someone who's gone out of her way to ruin my life.

"Take off your shirt and lie down on your stomach," she says.

I do, and she climbs on top of me. She's so light. Her smallness kind of fascinates me.

"Does this hurt you, Max?" She draws her fingers across my shoulder.

"No." It feels…good. I've never allowed anyone to

touch me before Peach and I'm still adjusting. With her, it's like the angst is laced with hope. It's an addictive feeling. Like a cool, clear stream running cheerfully through the raging fires of hell. I want to dive in and immerse myself in her. I don't ever want to be without her presence. I need it too much.

"How about this?" Her hands are delicate and careful, gliding and pressing in soft strokes.

I sigh without meaning to. Her hands continue to cool me, to sooth and to calm. I don't know how she does it. After all these years of despair, she lights up my life.

She plays with my hair and I feel myself drift. She's so gentle.

I feel calm and lucid, sort of enchanted with her effect.

The whispered words are so achingly beautiful, gliding through the mists of my haunted dreams.

You're good. You're mine. I love you, Max.

16

MAX SLEEPS in his bed with me all night. I watch over him and stay close to him. When he stirs, I calm him. I whisper love words, which quiet him. As I do, Max's face becomes peaceful. It brings tears to my eyes. Life has knocked him around and he struggles for air sometimes. He's been broken, but the heart of him beats with the purest kind of beauty I've ever known.

And I realize something: karma wasn't holding out on me by giving me reasons to question whether true love was worth the risk. Karma was making me wait. Karma was *delivering*. This big, scarred, beautiful man is *mine*. *He's* the one I've been waiting for all along. He's the one I saved myself for. It's *him*. It's been him since that very first moment.

He sleeps for fifteen hours and doesn't have a single nightmare.

In the morning, he wakes up early with me. It's Tuesday. Today is the day I go back to work.

The shadows under his eyes are practically gone. Not completely, but he doesn't look as tired. I still have a lot of fixing to do, but his angst is less pronounced today. This makes me immensely happy.

"That's the best night's sleep I've had in a very long time." His eyes gleam almost violet against the purple light of dawn.

He takes his gun out of its drawer and tucks it into the back of his jeans. I'm not as shocked this time. I'm glad he has it. *Just in case.*

We take the elevator down to ground level and walk out onto the street. It feels strange. Different. He brought me home three days ago, scared and lost. He took care of me. He shielded me. He made sure I was warm and safe. Somehow, he then showed me a side of myself I never knew about. Unwrapping parts of my body and soul like a budding flower that opens to the spring sun. And now that I'm enlightened in this way, I feel a deep sense of connection to him. After our cocooned days in his apartment, I don't want to be apart from him. It doesn't matter to me if his hacker listened or didn't listen. She can't break our bond. We won't let her.

It's a relief to me that Max seems to feel the same way.

As we walk out of his building, he holds my hand. "Okay?" he says, like he can sense my unease. I'm on the streets again, exposed. Visible to whoever might be looking for me.

My stalker has stolen something from me. He's shattered my blind, innocent sense of well-being.

But Max is with me. As long as he's here, I know I'll be okay.

"Should we walk?" I say. It's not far to my restaurant. Three blocks.

A limo pulls up. "My driver will take us."

This is going to take some getting used to. Luxury apartments, haute couture, limos: it's all just a little over-the-top.

We get to the restaurant and go inside. I lead him back to the kitchen. I put on a playlist and turn on the ovens. I put on my apron and start sprinkling flour onto the stainless steel table where I make the pies.

Max checks the back door to make sure it's locked and secure. He checks the corners and the walk-in chiller. For *him*, I guess. But it's just us.

He watches me roll the pastry dough for a while.

"Go find a table to work at, if you want, Max. I'm fine here. This is my happy place." Well, *one* of them, is what I'm thinking. I have a new happy place that's even happier than the kitchen, go figure. Anywhere Max Black happens to be.

He goes out and finds a table to sit at and I bring him some coffee and some warm apple pie with homemade ice cream for breakfast.

"You're a dream come true," he says. "My Georgia girl."

I smile, but I feel sort of stricken by his words. I *am* his. The extent of it is a little jarring. We've known each other for a short but very intense few days. And I can no longer imagine my life without him. Now I understand why they call it *falling* in love. You can't stop it from happening. And it only gains momentum the deeper you get. It makes me think of my parents. *I get it now,* I wish I could tell them. *It's worth whatever happens, just to try.*

I leave him to work and make phone calls and I lose myself for a while, as I tend to do when I cook or bake. Before I know it, Johnny and Sophie and some of my other staff are clocking in and putting on their aprons. I introduce them to Max and they all gush over him but I tell them to get to work. We open at twelve for lunch and Tuesdays are just as busy as any other day.

I go back to the kitchen and pull another batch of pies out of the oven. The clock says 10: 53. Sophie pokes her head into the kitchen. "Peach, Max wants you. Some-one's here to see you."

A wave of unease washes through me before I can stop it. *Max is here. You're safe.*

"Who is it?" I set the pies to cool and wipe my hands on my apron.

"Some real estate guy."

I go out to see Max. He's shaking hands with a middle-aged man dressed in a suit.

"Peach, this is Mr. Farrell. Mr. Farrell, Peach Sutton."

"Here are your keys, Miss Sutton," says Mr. Farrell. "And the titles for both properties. Congratulations."

"What properties?"

"This building. And the one across the street." Mr. Farrell seems confused by the fact that I have no idea what he's talking about. "You own them. Free and clear. The paperwork is complete."

"*Own* them?"

Mr. Farrell glances at Max, getting the gist of what's going on here. "I'll leave it up to Mr. Black to explain the particulars. Everything you need is in this envelope. There's also a list of contractors for the remodel. The wiring and plumbing were completely redone last year. And the appliances are all top-of-the-line. My card is in the envelope if you have any questions about anything. Sorry to cut this short, but I've got another appointment. Nice doing business with you, Mr. Black." He shakes Max's hand, then mine. "I wish you the very best with your new bakery, Miss Sutton. Enjoy your day."

With that, Mr. Farrell walks out.

Max is smiling at me, sort of deviously.

I glare at him, still processing everything Mr. Farrell just said. "Max? What is this?"

He takes my hand. "Let's go look at it."

Max pulls me out the door and we cross the street. He unlocks the carved wooden door and we go inside. The space is big, full of light from the large arched windows.

It's perfect, with industrial-sized ovens in the back and an etched glass display case that runs half the length of the room. There's enough floorspace for ten or twelve tables. "You *bought* this?" I'm still trying to figure out how I was going to afford to pay the deposit for a one-year rental lease.

He's smiling.

"Why?"

"I bought it for you."

I wonder if I've heard him correctly.

"And your restaurant premises, too. The whole building, in fact. There are four apartments on the other side of it I have a few ideas about what to do with. It's all yours."

"Max, you can't *buy* it."

"Of course I can. I already have. Everything's in your name."

"But—" My phone rings in my pocket. I pull it out. I'm going to have to tell Max he can't do all that. He'll have to give it back. It doesn't make any sense.

The screen reads *Grandma Bea*. Which is odd. She only calls me on Sundays.

"Hang on just a second." I feel a flare of panic as I answer the call. "Grandma Bea? Is everything all right?"

"Dixie May Rafferty Sutton, you are the biggest sweetheart in the whole wide world! I always knew you'd be the success story of this family. Lord above. You've got those money-making genes your granddaddy had. Too bad he gambled his fortune away, but never mind all that. They arrived at ten o'clock on the dot this morning, driving up out front with their fleet of blue vans. Me and the girls were having our tea on the porch and there we were, thinking, Who in tarnation *are* these people? Then, polite as can be, they start pulling their ladders and their work belts and their cans of paint out of their trucks and asking me where I want them to start. We're at your service, Miz Rafferty, says the foreman—his name's Ronnie and he's from Baton Rouge. Cute as a button. He said he got a phone call this morning and that he's here to do whatever I tell him for however long it takes. And then it clicked and I knew it must have been you who sent them. You always said you'd have this house fixed up for us as good as new, as soon as your restaurant was up and running. And I just wanted to call you and tell you how much I love you, honey. You're a darlin' and you always have been and I just don't know how to thank you. I better go now, honey. Ronnie has some questions. Call me later, when you have time. Oh, and Peach?"

"Yes?"

"When are you comin' home for a visit?"

"As soon as I can."

"All right. Thank you, darlin', from the bottom of my heart. Thank you so much. You won't even recognize the place by the time you get home. They're even going to fix up the cottage, your favorite place. We'll do everything up so pretty you'll hardly know it."

"I'm sure you will, Grandma Bea. I'll call you in a few days." I fight back tears. I'm not sure if they're tears of joy, homesickness or fury.

I end the call and turn to look at Max.

If I'm not mistaken, he looks guilty as sin. Like he's not sure how I'm going to take all this. And he's damn right to be uneasy. Because I'm not taking this well at all. "How *could* you?"

My hands are on my hips, which seems to amuse him. His uneasiness drifts, replaced by that assured arrogance that irks me. He's so damn smug.

"Calm down," he has the nerve to say.

"Calm *down*? I will *not* calm down! You know I'll never be able to pay you back for all this!"

"It's called a *gift*, Peach."

"A *gift*? It's too much of a gift! I don't want gifts! I want you to take your money back and stop giving me *gifts*. Right now! You need to undo all this before it goes too far, Max Black. I can let Grandma Bea down easy, today. Before she gets too used to the whole idea. And as for the restaurant and this bakery, you need to take it back. I won't accept it."

He's not smiling but he's got this self-satisfied smirk on his face that winds me up even more.

"Max?"

He walks over to the counter, surveying the space sort of dreamily.

"*Max.*"

"No."

"What do you mean, 'no'? I mean it! You need to start making some phone calls."

"Everything's already signed off," he says.

"Well, *un*sign it off."

"Peach, sweetheart, I'm not going to do that. So you might as well just get used to the idea."

"I will *not* get used to it!"

He laughs, the arrogant jerk.

"Fine. Be that way." I turn my back and storm out the door, across the street and into my restaurant. Max, irritatingly, has no trouble keeping up with me, and when I get to the tiny back office with its big desk and heavy door, because I need to be alone for a few minutes to figure out what to do, by the time I try to slam it, he's already pushing his way in there with me.

"Out," I say, but he's already in. And the door is closed. He locks it.

I'm flustered and upset. Emotions are coursing through my body faster than I can identify them. I miss Georgia. And Max shouldn't have done that.

"You had no right."

"Honey. Please. Let's take this down a notch. We can discuss this reasonably." He looks around. "You *sleep* in here?" His eyes rove to a stack of blankets and pillows in the corner, and the wildly uncomfortable sort-of reclining office chair. The office has room for the huge desk that I've occasionally wondered how they ever got it in here in the first place, the chair, and very little else.

I'm standing with my back against the door. Max is standing inches from me. Because there's nowhere else for him to stand. He sets the envelope he's holding onto the chair. He puts his palm flat on the door, caging me.

"I meant what I said," he says to me, all intensely. A lock of his hair sweeps across his forehead, dashingly. His dark gaze seems to pin me in place. His lips are close to mine.

"About what?"

He leans closer, like he's going to kiss me. But he doesn't. He makes me wait. "I said you're the most beautiful thing I've ever seen. I said I'm in love with you. I said that every second of every day I'll try my hardest to be good enough for you. I said I'll do anything and everything to keep you. I said I'm starved, obsessed and so hot for you that all I can think about is how I'm going to make you come again. Which is exactly what I'm about to do right now."

I'm speechless. I need to tone down the urges of my body. My heart is racing. My skin is flushed from my rage and his confessions and the warmth of his body so close to mine. His mouth is so deliciously enticing, I feel almost delirious with anticipation. But, *no*. He's taken liberties here he has no right to take.

Even so, his eyes are looking at me in that way again. That tender, adoring kindness he saves just for me.

"You don't need to buy me things to do all that, Max. You can show me by just being near me. By being there for me when I might need you." He's all around me, filling my senses with his man-scent and his beauty. "And by maybe kissing me sometimes."

Max smiles. Slowly, he leans closer, like he's teasing me. Then he kisses me like he's never kissed me before. His mouth is ravenous. His tongue pushes into me as his hands grip me, pulling my dress up. I'm wearing nothing underneath—he forgot about that detail in his most recent shopping spree and I've run out—and he drops to his knees. I grasp at his hair as he kisses my stomach, biting my skin, gripping hard with his fingers.

"Jesus Christ," he groans. "You are so damn beautiful."

Slowly, sweetly, he touches his mouth to my pussy, licking me with a long, slow stroke of his tongue.

My knees give out.

Max catches me, holding my weight like it's nothing. He lifts me and lays me onto the desk. He pulls my dress, which has elastic along the neckline, down over my breasts. "I'm going to kiss you all over, my sweet little Peach pie, and make you come. Are you ready for me?"

I'm breathing hard. I'm sprawled out under him with my dress pushed up—and down—so it's bunched around my waist. And I'm supposed to be mad at him.

He licks my nipple. "I'm not going to ask your permission every time I want to buy you something. I have shitloads of money. If I feel like buying you something, I'm going to fucking buy you something. Are we clear?"

He sounds like he means it. "I'm going to pay you back."

"You already did. When you served me a double slice of your pie. Warm with homemade ice cream on the side. And when you didn't walk out on me, even though I scared you and almost hurt you. You barely even flinched."

"Max, you didn't mean to do it."

"*I* know that. But you could've hated me for it."

"I couldn't hate you for that. It's not your fault."

He closes his eyes for a second. He exhales an exasperated little huff. Then his eyes open again and they're so full of emotion and love I don't ever want to look away. He's mine. My Max. "And *you* are more dazzling than anything my jaded mind could have dreamed up. Now stop protesting every damn thing. Lie back and let me give you what you need. Let me give you everything I have. It's the only thing that makes me feel good."

"Max?"

"Yeah?"

"I *am* going to pay you back. But thank you. For sending those contractors to my house. I want to take you down there. I want to show you the peach grove and my favorite little cottage in the rose garden."

"I can hardly wait. Now stop talking and close your eyes."

I do it. I close my eyes.

"Good girl. Now just relax." I do. I take a deep breath and let myself go. I give myself up to him. To whatever he's about to do.

He kisses my breasts. His strong, sure hands rove my body. His teeth close around my beaded nipple. The pressure sends tiny shards of pleasure to my core. It feels so good. I arch up to his mouth. I want his mouth on my body, on my skin. I moan, I can't help it. He sucks on my nipple, one then the other. Then he moves lower, pushing my dress up further, kissing and licking the skin of my stomach, my thighs, everywhere but where I want him.

I'm so wet. So *hot*. I need him.

I grab fistfuls of his hair. I feel frantic for him.

"I'm here, baby," he says against the wet skin of my thigh. "I'll give you everything you want. Just relax."

I do. I try. I'll do anything he says. *"Max."* I need him so much.

"Here I am, sweet girl."

His fingers touch me. His tongue licks me. He laps tenderly at first, dipping his tongue inside me with tender, prodding strokes. His fingers ease inside as his mouth latches onto my clit, sucking and flicking in tugging little pulls, so adoringly. I squirm, but he holds me in place with his hands, doing whatever he wants with me. His mouth licks into me, sucking strongly on my clit as his fingers prod deeper. He holds me down. His mouth is greedy and relentless. Licking me *everywhere*. Max Black has never heard of Southern manners, that's for damn sure. *Thank God.*

Oh, sweet Jesus.

His mouth is pulling, teasing, eating me alive.

I can feel it starting. The sweet heat is rising. He won't relent. He can tell I'm starting to come. He unzips himself and lays over me, sliding his cock thickly into me, forcefully, and it feels crazy-good. The wave rises so fast and crashes so hard I think I might be moaning or crying or begging for him to stop and also keep going. I can feel the zinging jolt all the way to my fingers and toes. The center of me is pulsing with ecstasy. I'm writhing and squirming. I think I might be telling him I love him. Because I do.

The waves start to calm. I try to catch my breath. I wait for my heartbeat to level out.

But then he thrusts again and I feel his cock jerk inside me as his fingers play me so sweetly I want to cry. Max groans like his heart's being pulled out of his chest and I feel it then: the warm, thick jets of his cum deep inside my body, filling me. I come again. Even harder. The pulsing beauty is too much. The swell is excruciating. I can only ride it, and wonder if I'll ever recover from this.

I'm grasping his hair in silky handfuls. I'm crying his name.

I'm never giving him up. I'm never letting him go. My

lover is some sort of sensual genius. A magician and a work of art, all rolled into one.

In time, I come down. Reality starts to ease its way in.

He gazes into my eyes. He kisses me, answering all my deepest desires, making all my dreams feel real and true and so, so beautiful.

"*Max.*"

"Right here, baby."

It's all I'm capable of, so I say, "Mine."

He's smiling that smug smile again and this time I'll admit it's warranted. "All yours, Peach pie. All yours."

17

I'VE FOUND HEAVEN on earth and it's right here. My sweet little Georgia girl.

I swore off close physical contact years ago and never expected to have much to do with it. I accepted, as part of my damages, that it was just who I was. This, now, *her*: I can't get close *enough*. She's so goddamn gorgeous, the edges of my sanity feel frayed by the magnitude of it.

Both of our phones are ringing. We ignore them. My pact with Rafe is going to need some new goddamn ground rules.

I'm on top of Peach, doing my best to hold my weight but I'm basically pinning her to the desk. Her dress is bunched up, her legs wrapped around me. My cock is wedged deeply inside her, hard again. My fingers are slippery, engaged in all kinds of debauchery, playing out the lingering ripples of her release. Her eyes are lust-drowsed and dreamy, gazing into mine with wonder. Almost like I'm too good to be true. Our bodies are still locked in a secret, lingering rhythm. We just came ridiculously hard.

"I can't believe I found you," I whisper, awed, hoping my words can imprint her body and soul with my wild passion and my vast, total devotion.

Her long eyelashes blink at me. She looks so beautiful all sated and peaceful it makes me crazy. I want to pick her up and carry her off into the sunset.

"You…" she says, soft and quietly accusing. "…are some kind of genius, Max Black. Raunchy as hell, but a genius. I don't even want to know how you got so damn *good* at that."

I've forgotten everything before her. Long-ago memories don't interest me. My dark past is exactly where it belongs: in the past.

She's looking at me like *that* again: like she sees something in me no one else ever has. Like I'm gallant and strong and extraordinary. I've never felt like any of those things before. Until now. With her, I *want* to be those things. I want to be everything she deserves.

Slowly, I start to disengage, even though I don't want to. "Come with me tonight," I say. "I need you close by."

"Of course I'll come with you, Max. I'll just have to ask my staff to cover for me again, but I'm sure they won't mind."

I finally found what I never thought I would and I'm not about to share her with every idiot who wants to order a slice of pie. "I've set up some appointments for you this week. You need more staff. Especially since you'll be running the bakery now, too. I'm flying a few people in to interview with you. Bakers and chefs from the top culinary schools in France and a couple of rising stars from around the U.S. They start arriving tomorrow. You're going to hire as many people as you need and you're going to start delegating. So you don't have to work such long hours anymore. You're the owner and the executive of this business. Which means you don't have to work every hour of every day. That's what staff is for."

She blinks at me. Her eyes are starry.

"I know what it's like to be a workaholic because I am one. Or at least I was one. Now I have other things to do that are more important. *One* other thing, more accurately. Spending all my time with my wild little strawberry-blond goddess."

"But—"

I rest my finger against her lips, to silence her. "You'll bake when you want to bake. You'll oversee, rather than working the floor all the time."

I use the blanket to wipe away the wetness of our lovemaking. I help her sit up. I pull her dress back down and try to smooth it into place.

"Did you just say there are people flying in from *France* to interview with me?"

"Yes. And Chicago. And New York."

"But…how did you organize all that so fast? And everything else, too? The bakery. The restaurant."

"I'm rich, so people do whatever I tell them."

She rolls her eyes. "Max, you can't keep buying me all these outrageous things and organizing everything in my life. You just can't."

"Why not?"

"Because. You don't need to."

"I want to." I almost feel hurt, which is fucked. I didn't even think I was *capable* of feeling hurt. It's been a long time since an actual emotion has even shown up on my radar. My emotions basically flatlined around thirteen years ago, until Peach walked in. So this rush of feeling… it kind of floors me.

She looks at me with exasperation. Then her expression changes, and softens. I was expecting protests, so I'm relieved she's not going to fight me this time. "I want to spend time with you because I like you for who you are. Not because of your money. In fact I wish you'd stop throwing it around like you're some kind of sugar daddy on steroids."

"I just want to make you happy," I say. It sounds cheesy as fuck but it's true.

She holds my face in her hands. She kisses me. Then she smiles. "You act all tough. You *look* all tough. But you're gooey and sweet on the inside, like a big roasted marshmallow."

"I'm not sure I like that analogy."

She laughs. "You will when I start eating you."

I stare at her. I'm so fucking in love with her I almost hold her down and ravage her all over again. She's smiling and giggling at me like a mischievous little nymphet.

I grab her and she laughs and squirms. She puts a finger to my lips and I keep still. I'll listen to anything she says. I'll do anything she asks. "Let me go. I need to help out my staff. They're being run off their feet and it's not fair that I'm in here having multiple orgasms while they're slaving away."

"All right. But I'm going to watch you while you work and fantasize about what I'm going to do to you later. Because I haven't even gotten started."

Her blue eyes widen. Her lips part. "Neither have I," she whispers.

I take her lower lip very lightly between my teeth.

She pulls away. "Let me go."

I obey. I help her up and smooth her hair back into place. I zip up and do my best to look presentable.

We leave the office and she blows me a kiss as she disappears into the kitchen. Before the door closes I see her staff flock around her. At first it takes me a second to identify the ache in my chest. Of longing. I'm *jealous*, that's what this is. I feel lost, having to share her.

So I moodily take up residence in my corner booth, trying to distract myself with work. I start checking my messages. Rafe has left five. Jesus.

I call him.

"Why the fuck haven't you been answering?"

"I was busy."

Silence. Like it's finally occurring to him *why* I might have been busy. He can be incredibly fucking dense sometimes for a billionaire CEO. "How's Peach?"

What to say? Ridiculously flawless. Off-the-charts sexy. So damn tasty it'll blow your head off. "Fine."

"That's good."

"Why are you calling?"

I can hear in his voice that he's entertained by the fact that I'm not about to spill a single detail. I have a serious urge to punch him. "You ready for tonight?"

"No." I really don't want to do what I'm about to do. Surely Melanie must suspect something. I already know what she's capable of, and that she's unpredictable. The whole thing feels risky. Too risky.

"It'll be okay, Max," Rafe says. I wonder if it will. I feel a million miles from okay. I have no patience for any of this. My fury has taken on a new gleam: to get rid of these people who are interfering with us. At any cost. "Charlie's a genius at this shit. I'm sure it'll all go smoothly and we'll get what we need. We'll see you there at four."

I agree, and end the call.

I look up to see Peach setting down a plate of French onion soup and a slice of freshly baked bread with melted butter. She's smiling at me. "In case you worked up an appetite." Her skin is luminous. Coiling tendrils frame her face. Her eyes gleam that surreal shade of periwinkle blue. She looks otherworldly, she's so pretty.

Fuck everything.

My voice sounds rasped when I tell her: "If anything goes wrong tonight, or if I somehow end up getting thrown in jail anyway, I just want you to know that the past three days have been the best of my life. I'll make sure you're safe, no matter what happens."

She's watching me, tuning into my pain and my regret. She sits next to me and takes my hand.

I pull the key card to my apartment out of my pocket. And the number of my driver. I slide them into the pocket of her apron. I'm about to tell her I love her again, when I notice the terrified look on her face.

"Max. *Look*."

I follow her gaze. Across the street, a cop car has pulled up. The doors open.

And I know who they're coming for.

If I told you to buy shares now because their value will skyrocket after the takeover and then advised you sell those shares at a huge profit the week after that…that would be insider trading.

Me.

I GRAB PEACH'S HAND. We run to the kitchen.

"Johnny!" says Peach urgently. "We need to borrow

your car to get out to Malibu. Is it parked in the back alley?"

Johnny takes off his apron. "I'm coming with you."

"I'll drive," I say, and the way I say it leaves no doubt. Johnny hands me his keys and we slip out the back door.

There's a red mustang sitting there—not the newest model, but probably only three or four years old. "Nice ride, man." I slide into the driver's seat. "Buckle up."

"Thanks," Johnny says. "Charlie bought it for me."

We clear the alley before the back door of the restaurant opens, and I take a right, then left, before weaving my way through a few side streets to get to the highway. It's not long before we're heading north on 1. They'll be able to track me, but for now, we're clear.

MELANIE ARRIVES EARLY, but by then, the place is set up, a wire is sewn into my collar and the champagne is on ice.

I kissed Peach for a long time before I let her go upstairs, where Rafe and Charlie and Johnny are waiting in the upstairs lounge, out of sight. "Get what you need," she whispered, "then come back to me." I could see on her face that she's worried, scared and maybe even a little jealous, in a careful, understanding way. A very *Peach* kind of way. The fact that she has to feel anything at all that has to do with this debacle is just wrong.

This whole thing is testing the limits of what I can tolerate. I just hope I can be civil.

I open the door for Melanie and there she is, dressed in a skin-tight black dress. It's been months since I last saw her and I'd forgotten the defining features of her face. Some might call her pretty in an overly made up, spray-tanned, plasticky sort of way, but to me she looks grating and harsh. Maybe because I know what she's capable of. She may as well be the devil standing there in her pointy stilettos and her low-cut dress. I feel like slamming the door in her face, but then I notice she's carrying her laptop.

Bingo.

"Hi, Max," she purrs. "Thank you so much for inviting me." She looks around and, as I open the door wider, steps inside. "This place is amazing. Is it yours?"

"Yes." It's Rafe's, but she'll feel more at home if she thinks it's mine. "I'm glad you could make it."

She notices the bottle of champagne in its ice bucket. "Is this for us?"

"I thought we could walk down to the beach and have a drink before we talk business. It's been a while since we've seen each other."

"That sounds perfect. It's such a nice night."

I open the bottle and pour two glasses, as we ignore the elephant in the room. *She maliciously plotted and schemed to get me incarcerated for up to ten years.* I'm tempted to chug the whole fucking thing, to calm my frayed nerves.

"Max Black," she smiles, checking me out, "as handsome as ever. You look like you've been working out a lot."

I take a step back before she can reach out to feel my bicep, which she's eyeing. I'm used to women trying to touch me. And I'm well-practiced at avoiding contact.

She licks her lips and takes a sip of her drink, leaving a bright red smear on the glass. I'll have to remember to smash that one. "I just want to start by saying that I know I've behaved badly, Max. And I'm sorry." *For which part? Hacking into my email address? Almost getting me thrown in jail? Or listening in on the most intimate and beautiful conversations I've ever had, with a woman who showed me exactly why I couldn't settle for someone like you?* "I wanted so badly to see you again. I mean, we had that incredible night together and then, well, you just…left. You wouldn't answer my letters or my calls. It seemed really unfair."

Keep your cool, Max. Keep your eye on the ball and say whatever needs to be said. "It was rude of me. I got caught up with work and so on."

"And so on," she repeats. "I hear you've been spending time with the owner of that new restaurant. What's her name?"

I can't bring myself to say it. I don't even want the word hanging in the air, anywhere near this viper. I don't want any part of *her* touching any part of Peach. The fact that Melanie knows as much as she does, *because she planted ten fucking bugs in my apartment,* makes me momentarily speechless with rage.

I do my best to recover. I grab the bottle of champagne. "Let's go. There's a path out here that leads down to the beach. We can talk there."

She starts following me, carrying all her stuff.

I try to sound casual. "You can leave your bags here. They'll be safe. And we won't be long."

She sets her purse and her laptop on a chair. I can't believe this is working. She's falling for it, hook, line and sinker. It doesn't surprise me that she'll do whatever I ask. That she probably knows what she's risking to spend time with me. It's the way women have reacted to me since I hit puberty.

Except for one, who needs to be convinced. Who gets mad at me when I buy her gifts in my attempt to do anything to keep her. But then she forgives me, in the sweetest, sexiest way imaginable.

Now all I have to do is put up with a twenty minute conversation with this evil bitch, and maybe—just maybe—I'll be free of her, once and for all. Maybe Peach and I *can* get our happy ever after. If I can just survive the next twenty minutes…maybe we can.

I lead Melanie down to the beach, which takes a while because her heels are fucking ludicrous. She almost catapults down the flight of three steps and I'm forced to grab her arm to stop her from falling. I remove my touch as soon as she's stable, and it leaves me hollow-feeling in its aftermath. Touching her makes it feel like the doom is returning. That sense of dread that has hounded me my whole life and that only lifts when Peach is near me, like sun burning through fog. I miss her so much I want to fucking punch something. Instead, I keep going. So I can get back to her as soon as possible.

The sun is hanging low in the sky, reflecting off the water. I put a blanket on the sand and we sit.

"Never picked you for a romantic, Max. This is so nice."

Yes. As nice as a sting operation can be—one that's designed to duplicate the contents of your computer, trace the origins of the anchor you planted, and incriminate you so thoroughly we can put you away for years if we choose to.

I try to think of something to say. "I like it down here at this time of the day." Cheesy, but she smiles.

"I hadn't forgotten how gorgeous you are…but, *wow*, is all I can say. Even my memories—which are fairly detailed—don't do you justice."

I'm not sure how to reply to that, so I don't.

"The time off from work seems to be agreeing with you," she comments blithely.

This is harder than I thought it was going to be. It takes every ounce of self-control I possess not to react. *She*, of course—this raving lunatic in siren-red lipstick—is the very *reason* I've been forced to take time off. Because everyone at my company thinks I'm a goddamn criminal.

"I'll send an email to the judge tomorrow," she says. Here we go. I can only hope and pray the wire Charlie put into my shirt collar is doing its job. "Clearing you of everything. I just…I want another night with you first, Max."

Wow. So blackmail is next on the list.

"Once you find out what I'm willing to *do*, Max, I'm sure…well, I just *know* we're supposed to be together. I can feel it."

My reply isn't quite as nice as I'm going for. "It's too bad you have to threaten me with extended prison time to try to get me into bed, Melanie. Honesty and integrity would have been so much more effective." I'm trying to keep this exchange as smooth as possible, but my nerves are tightly wound. This chick has put me through hell.

And if the way she's twirling the long strand of her hair is anything to go by, she has every intention of *continuing* to put me through hell. Until she gets exactly what she wants. "I tried honesty. Those letters were heartfelt."

"The ones with the bugs sewn into them?"

"I only did that later, Max. After I'd sent you dozens and you never—not once—replied to me."

If I'd wanted to reply, I would have replied, is on the tip of my tongue, but I don't want her storming back up to the house in a huff. Not yet, at least. Not until I get what I need and Charlie gets what he needs.

She moves a fraction closer. "It could be so *good* between us, if you'd just give me another chance. Why don't we go back up to the house so I can show you…*how* good?"

Fuck this. Charlie, hurry the fuck up.

I can't risk interrupting him too soon.

So I top up our glasses. "Let's watch the sunset first."

She takes another sip of champagne. "Max. I really am sorry. I was really hurt when you ignored me like that. I guess I just wanted to even the score a little. Is that so hard to understand?"

"So you got me convicted of a federal offense I didn't commit. That feels a little…*un*even."

"I was upset! You humiliated me."

She's admitting she framed me. I'm getting it all on tape. For the first time since my arrest, I feel the tiniest glimmer of hope. "I didn't humiliate you. We shared some time and then I left."

"It was the best three hours of my life."

I stare at her. *Seriously?* It was among the *worst* three hours of mine. Because, strangely, I could almost sense what was coming. Just a little too late.

"I mean, holy hell." She exhales a small laugh. "You're so unbelievably good in bed. No other man has ever been able to——"

"Melanie. Listen. Whatever happened between us is over. It's not going to happen again. Not tonight. Not ever."

She stares at me, actual tears pooling in her eyes. "How can you say that? I would never have let them send you to prison, Max. I would have cleared your name before they locked you up."

As great as all this confession bullshit might be, I can't help myself. "How fucking considerate of you."

She's shocked by the sting of my comment, which, after all she's done to me, is sort of ridiculous. "I didn't *plan* on framing you. It was the only way I could get your attention."

"Bail cost me six million dollars. That definitely got my attention."

"They'll give it all back once I send a few emails."

Surely I've got enough by now. Does Charlie? "You ruined my reputation."

"I'll fix it."

She's so fucking smug about whatever power or sway she thinks she has over my life. This enrages me beyond belief. How can anyone be so bold and abrasive and fucked? "This isn't a game, Melanie. This is my *life* you're playing with."

Her expression changes. To one of sadness. "I know. I'm sorry." Her voice has lost its steely edge. She's playing a different card: the helpless female, jilted by an unfeeling asshole like me. "You broke my heart," she sobs. Tears draw shiny lines down her cheek, smearing her make-up. "I *want* you, Max, more than I've ever wanted anything. That's why I went to such extremes. Because I *love* you."

I stand up. The words jar me, because I don't want to hear them from her. There's only one person I want to hear those words from, and I can't take another second of this. Not when I should be with Peach, showering her with gifts and showing her what real love is. A million miles from this twisted, toxic thing going on here and now.

"Let's go back up to the house," I say, dully, and her eyes light up.

She wipes her tears, smearing her makeup further. "We can work this out, Max. I know we can."

Charlie, you better be fucking finished, because I'm done.

Faintly, in the distance, I hear sirens.

I don't bother offering her my arm as I walk up the stone steps. If she touches me again, I don't know how I'll react.

"I promise I'll make everything up to you, Max." She's pleading, clambering after me. "I'll make you feel so good you'll *have* to forgive me. You'll see."

None of that's going to happen. Because everything about you is exactly what I've been trying for years to avoid. And because whenever I'm near you, all I can feel is the layers of my despair and the very worst of myself.

She starts to reach for me. Her fingertips graze my shirt.

A wave of disgust floods through me. All that old rage and fear and sadness and shame erupts in some crazy overwrought reaction I'm not expecting. I recoil. I back away. My hands are raised in front of me like I'm ready for a fight. If she touches me I'll do something violent, I can feel it.

The sound of sirens is getting louder.

I would rather face my fate, whatever it might be, than endure even one more second of this.

"Max? Please. *Max.*"

"*Stay away from me,*" I growl under my breath and my voice sounds cold, iced by those deep damages, the darkest places I know. "Throw me to the wolves if that's your thing. Ruin my life. But don't ever, ever touch me."

I walk up to the house in ground-eating strides.

I can see the flashing lights of the cop cars, now parked out in front of Rafe's house. They've come for me. *Do we have enough to clear me? Or don't we? What if we don't?*

There's one more thing I need to take care of. I make my way toward the house.

I can practically feel the doom and the prison walls closing in.

MAX STORMS in through the open French doors, at exactly the same time Rafe opens the door to the pounding of the police officers. Max looks shaken and furious, with that same empty look in his eyes he had that night when the nightmares woke him. All I want to do is go to him and comfort him. I know now: *I'm his haven, just like he's mine. I can ease his anguish like no one else. If only they would leave us alone.*

But he's followed closely by Melanie, whose makeup is smeared under her eyes in heavy black smudges.

Four armed officers rush in through the door. "We have a warrant for the arrest of Mr. Maximillian A. Black. Which one of you is Max Black?"

"Right here," says Max, walking straight over to Rafe and grabbing fistfuls of the front of Rafe's shirt. "Keep her *safe*, Rafe. I'm fucking *ordering* you to protect her with your life."

"Max," Rafe says, putting his hands on Max's shoulders, in a brotherly gesture that's almost a hug. "You're going to do that yourself, with my help. We got all of it. The confession on tape, the duplicate of all the files, the email trace. Everything."

Max glances at the cops, who are all carrying guns and wearing full body armor. Then he glances back at Rafe. Then Charlie. Finally…me. His expression softens and a visceral current passes between us. *God, I love him.* "You did?" he says.

"We did," Charlie confirms. "Officers, we have extensive evidence to prove that this man is innocent of all charges."

"What do you mean?" shrieks Melanie, rushing over to her laptop, which is now back on the chair, exactly as she left it. Well, not *exactly*. I watched as Charlie hacked into it, duplicated everything and confirmed the origin of the email she sent to Max. He told me he'd played back the recordings from the bugs Melanie planted in Max's home office—which turned out to have very little on them. Turns out the bugs were muted by all the shredded paper and the glass walls of Max's office. And then there was the recorded conversation they just had on the beach—which was very hard to listen to. He sounded so sad. Which makes me furious. *How dare she fuck with him like that?* "This is private property!"

"So was mine," says Max.

Melanie moves toward Max, as though to lash out at him. Before she can get close to him, I step in her way. She stops and stares at me, with her fists balled. "This has nothing to do with you," she says, ice practically dripping off her words.

"Wrong. This has everything to do with me. He has enough to put you away for years. You're lucky he's kind. *I'm* not as forgiving, so if you so much as touch him, I'm going to make sure Max prosecutes you to the full extent of the law. And I can be very persuasive when I put my mind to it." We're staring at each other and it's strange. I'm not a confrontational person, but I can feel my blood coursing through my veins and it's hot. I'm not letting her near him. "Right, Max?"

I glance at him. Max is looking at me with an expression that, despite everything that's going on around us, makes my stomach do a flip. It's a look that's…*hot as fuck.* "Sure is."

Melanie glares at Max, and she breaks down. Tears have already destroyed her makeup and it's only getting worse. "You won't get away with this!"

"Miss Ames?" says one of the officers, gesturing with his big gun to Melanie. "I'm going to need you to come over here and take a seat."

Johnny, who's been fluttering around at somewhat of a loose end all afternoon, offers Melanie a Kleenex and helps her over to a couch, where she proceeds to have a total meltdown, to him, the only one who will listen.

It takes a while, but Rafe and Charlie and Max explain everything to the officers. We all end up going down to the police station where we give statements.

Melanie is placed under arrest—not at all willingly. She's a hot mess by the time they drag her off to her cell, pleading with Max to forgive her.

The police chief shakes his head a little. He takes off Max's cuff. "There'll be a hearing, but you're no longer under house arrest," he says to Max. "Looks like you've been through hell."

"You could say that." He squeezes my hand. "But it was worth it."

It occurs to me that, without Melanie's interference, Max might never have come to my restaurant that very first night I met him. He came because it was in his zone. And then he came back.

The police chief glances at me before shaking Max's hand. "You have a good night, now," he says. "You're free to go."

19

THE RELIEF IS SORT OF indescribable. We're in Rafe's limo, getting a ride back to my apartment. I hold Peach's hand all the way. We don't say much. We'll have to decide how hard we want to prosecute, but we've been advised to give it a day or two to think about it. I've already decided. I'll forgive, under one condition. That Melanie never contacts, sees or so much as thinks about me or Peach ever again for the rest of time.

It's five a.m. We've been at the police station all night.

We pull to a stop along a side street near the entrance to my private elevator. Rafe gives me a man-hug. "Told you," he says.

I exhale a short laugh. "You're always right."

"Call me tomorrow." Rafe gives Peach a hug, too. "Take good care of him."

"I will, Rafe."

We get out, and the limo pulls away and turns a corner.

As I'm reaching into my pocket for my electronic key, a white van pulls up. There's no one else on the street.

A man steps out of the driver's door and my blood goes cold.

It's *him.*

It's Peach's stalker. He's wearing a sweatshirt with the hood up, covering some of his face.

He's holding a gun.

"You think I'd be that easy to get rid of?" he says in a low, eerie voice. "I found out who you were. Where you live. I've been watching you. I've been waiting for you two to get home."

I start reaching for my gun, but he raises his.

"Keep your fucking hands where I can see them, man," he hisses.

Peach makes a light noise, of panic, and I step in front of her. "*Max, no.*"

"She's coming with me," says the thug. His finger is on the trigger of his handgun, which he points straight at my chest.

"That's not happening," I tell him.

He laughs and the sound is sinister. This man is twisted and sadistic, you can hear that. This man is capable of terrible things. "I've got a real itchy finger, so don't try me. I'm going to take her, and you're going to let me."

"I'll give you money. As much as you want. Name your price."

"Oh, I'll get money. But first I want the girl."

Over my dead body. "No."

"I've got some things planned for us," he says.

"Ten million. I can get it now. You can walk away."

"The girl. Give her to me."

"Take me instead. Twenty million. A hundred."

I can see on his face that he's too doomed to bargain. Maybe he's killed before. Something behind his eyes is already dead. "I'll fucking shoot you, man. Give her to me."

He takes a step forward. I reach for my gun and pull it out, flicking off the safety.

Before I can fire my gun, I hear a noise. It's not as loud as you'd expect, but you can feel the impact. Deeply.

Peach screams.

I don't even feel the pain of it, just the heat. It's fucking *hot*. And then I feel the spreading warmth of my own blood. The ground rushes up to meet me and *I can't let this happen. I'm her shield. I need to fucking kill him.* She's screaming and pulling open my shirt. Her hands are red. If only she didn't look so upset. I can't have my girl crying like this. I try to tell her everything's okay. But before I can—even though I'm trying like fuck to find my gun and hang on to her, the world goes black.

20

"*No*. Max. *Max*." The bullet has gone into the side of his stomach and I can't see if it's come out. I swipe away my tears and try to get a better look. It's a small, neat hole, pooling with rivers of blood. *There's so much blood.* It's coming too quickly. I bunch up a wad of his shirt and hold it onto the hole, applying pressure. "*Max*." He's bleeding to death.

I don't even think about it. I pick up Max's gun, which is next to his hand where he dropped it, and in one quick motion I take aim and at the same time I pull the trigger. It almost seems to be happening in slow motion. I watch the bullet hit the stalker, who's close to me now. *Take that, you fucker.* It hits him right in the middle of his chest, spraying blood. He's not expecting it. He stares at me for a second, surprised, then he falls backward. His body jerks lightly and then he goes completely still. A pool of blood spills onto the sidewalk in a thick, creeping stain underneath him. He doesn't move again.

Holy fuck.

I just shot him. I think I just killed that man.

I turn back to Max.

I manage to take my phone out of my pocket. There's hardly any battery left. Why is it so wet? I dial 911. "Hello? I need an ambulance. *Please.* Max Black has been shot. He's bleeding. Please, *please* hurry." I give the address and the woman on the phone tells me to stay with him, that help is coming, that I need to stay calm. My phone goes dead.

I put more pressure on his wound. "You're going to be fine, Max," I hear myself saying. "You stay with me, Max Black. I love you. I need you. We're going to get our happy ever after, do you hear me? You're going to be okay and I'm going to take you to Georgia to show you the peach orchards. We're going to get married and have our honeymoon in New Orleans. We're going to have lots of babies and grow old together, okay? So you need to listen to what I'm telling you and hold on. Just hold on, Max. *Please.* Everything will be okay, you'll see." My tears are dripping onto him, mixing with his blood.

It feels like an eternity, but the ambulance arrives and someone pulls me away from him so they can put him on a stretcher.

There's commotion surrounding the other man lying

on the sidewalk. I hear someone pronounce him dead. They put a sheet over him.

"I shot him," I tell them.

They seem shocked by this, as I guess they should be. It's hard to get any sense of reality.

I'm not leaving Max. They allow me to climb into the ambulance and sit close to him as they work on him, as they put needles into his arm and put clean bandages on his wound, pressing on it. I keep talking to him, all the way to the hospital. I know he can hear me. *Please, Max. Please hear me. You have to.*

When we get to the hospital, they wheel him away into the operating room and the police are waiting for me. "I need to call Rafe," I tell them. The officer lets me use his phone. I google Downtown and call the number.

A receptionist answers. "Downtown, how can I help?"

"I need Rafe Black's personal number immediately."

"I'm sorry, he's unavailable. Would you like to leave a message for one of his secretaries?"

"It's an emergency. Please. It's Rafe's brother, Max. He's been shot."

"What? Oh my God. Is he okay?"

"I don't know." I swipe at my tears.

"Hold on just a second. I'll get you Rafe's number."

She gives me the number and I call Rafe.

He answers on the first ring. "Rafe Black." Rafe's voice sounds like Max's. It's got that husky edge to it.

My eyes start overflowing again. "Rafe? It's Peach. Max…he's been shot."

His split-second pause is electric with panic. "*What?*"

"We're at the hospital. They're operating." I can barely even say it. "I don't know if he's okay, Rafe. There was so much—" My throat works hard and I can't speak.

"Peach, what hospital are you at? I'm coming now. Just tell me where you are."

I look up at the sign and tell him the name.

"I'm on my way."

So I sit there and wait and let the tears fall. There are so many of them. I can't seem to slow them down. That bullet was *my* fault. He took it for me.

The officers start questioning me—for the second time in less than twelve hours—and I tell them everything I can remember. Someone puts a blanket around me and I realize I'm shaking.

Rafe rushes in and I stand up. He puts his hands on my shoulders. "Where is he?" His voice catches as he asks the question.

"He's still in surgery. The bullet went into his stomach." I'm crying again and Lexi's here, too. She's hugging me and smoothing my hair.

"I'm going to go see what I can find out," says Rafe.

Lexi takes me into the bathroom and cleans me up a little. She washes my face. She takes a top out of her bag and helps me change into it. I didn't even realize my clothes were literally soaked with Max's blood.

When we get back to the waiting room, Rafe's there. "The bullet didn't exit. They can't tell us any more than that until the doctors are finished operating."

He goes and gets us some coffee and I tell them what happened.

"Shit," Rafe says.

We wait.

Goddamn him, he can't *die* on me. He's the *one*. I need him to *live*. The hot, silent tears just keep on falling.

After what seems like several lifetimes, a doctor walks down the hall and into the waiting room. We all stand up. "It grazed his liver. We've taken out his spleen, which was ruptured. He has two broken ribs. The entry wound itself was fairly clean and there was no exit wound so the suturing was fairly straightforward. It'll take a while to heal, but he should make a full recovery."

I'm so relieved my knees sort of give out and I sit down on my chair. Rafe shakes the doctor's hand.

"He's still in recovery but he can have visitors once he wakes up," the doctor tells us. "Go home and eat something. Come back around six o'clock."

Rafe and Lexi take me back to their apartment. I take a shower and Lexi gives me some clean clothes to wear. None of us say much. I think we're so relieved, we're all a little overcome by it. *He should make a full recovery.* This realization is so profound to me I feel like I've been completely torn apart and reassembled. My pieces fit together differently now. Everything has become about being with Max and getting our happy ever after. That's all I want to do.

When we finally arrive back at the hospital Max has been moved to a private room. He's awake, propped up in a reclining hospital bed in his hospital gown with his cuts and bruises and his muscles and tattoos. He looks so gorgeous I can hardly breathe.

Rafe gives him a brotherly hug and swears at him in the most endearing way I've ever heard, for giving us such a fright. Lexi kisses his cheek.

"Okay, you two," Max says. "Back off. I need to see my girl."

I hold Max's face in my hands and kiss a cut on his cheekbone. "You scared me," I tell him.

"You shot him?"

My tears just won't quit. I'm glad the stalker is gone. I know it was self-defense and the threat was real and too horrible to think about, but it's still a very heavy thing to have done. "Yes."

"Sometimes we have to do whatever it takes to survive," he says, repeating the words I said to him once, when he first began to trust me with the things about his past that haunted him the most.

I kiss his lips gently, so I don't hurt him.

A nurse is checking one of his machines. "You'll compromise his recovery if you keep that up." She winks at me.

But Max doesn't seem to hear. He reaches up to hold

me there, even as he winces. "Peach pie?"

"Yes, Max." I'm kissing him and he smiles. I love his smile. I love his face and his eyes and his kiss.

With Rafe and Lexi and two nurses listening in, which Max doesn't even notice, he says, "As soon as I get out of here, I'm taking you down to Tiffany's and you're going to choose any ring you want. Then we're going to Georgia to get married in that peach orchard you keep going on about. And after that, we're going to New Orleans. Please marry me, Peach, so I can give you the best happy ever after you could ever imagine. Please say yes."

Our happiness will always have layers of sorrow and regret. But the way I see it, the sun always shines just a little brighter after the rain. I cry some more and I kiss him again. "Yes, Max. Yes."

EPILOGUE

MAX GETS DISCHARGED from the hospital three weeks later. Even though I try to stop him, he's been making a lot of phone calls and working from his hospital bed.

He still has to take it easy and I suggest we go back to his apartment so he can rest for a while, but he insists on taking me straight to the restaurant. The bakery is almost ready and we've planned a grand opening once we get back from our honeymoon. All the people Max flew in for job interview were hired—Johnny and Sophie ended up interviewing most of them—so my staff has more than doubled. Which means I can delegate. Max insisted (and paid a full year of their salary, which I wasn't happy about. But he just smiled and I somehow ended up forgiving him).

"I've been resting for three weeks. I can't take any more rest. Besides, there's something I want to show you."

He leads me to a side door around the corner from the entrance to the restaurant that always used to be locked. It has new steps and a new door. Max has a key. He opens the door and we step into an airy foyer with an elevator. He presses the button and the elevator door opens.

"I never even knew this was here."

"It wasn't."

I give him a look. "Max? What is this?"

"I haven't exactly been doing nothing for the past three weeks," he says. "I've been managing a very exclusive project. They've put it together amazingly quickly. Then again, practically every contractor in town's been working on it. I think you're going to like this." I had noticed a lot of people coming and going around the back, but thought it was construction in the next building.

The elevator door opens.

We step out into the most beautiful space I've ever seen. It's an apartment—a huge, open-plan apartment with a two-story glassed-in greenhouse in the middle with a domed top. In the greenhouse is a rose garden surrounded by five fully-mature peach trees. They even have peaches on them. The windows of the greenhouse open to the apartment itself.

"I had all of it shipped from your orchards and gardens in Georgia. With strict instructions from Grandma Bea, of course, and her friends. They were sworn to secrecy. She's coming up this weekend for a visit, by the way. To make sure I've done it justice."

But I'm too mesmerized by this beautiful apartment to fully take in what he's saying. It has clean white walls with black accents and lots of wood. Sophisticated details are everywhere. A huge chef's kitchen fills one entire corner. There's a long dining table with ten chairs that looks out the windows over the views of the city, all the way to the ocean. There's a great room with a big-screen TV and huge, comfortable-looking couches.

"Let's go see the bedrooms," he says, leading me into the garden, where there's a grand, curving staircase. "There's also an elevator."

Upstairs there are five bedrooms. The master suite has a king-sized bed that looks like it could sleep an entire family, an enormous walk-in closet and a master bathroom made of marble and stone, with just the right touches of wood and fabric to soften the look, giving it an opulent, romantic feel. "I've never seen anything like this."

"It's for you," he says. Then he leads me back to the greenhouse and he gets down onto one knee. He takes a small duck-egg blue box out of his pocket. "I want to do this properly, without an audience and without the hospital gown. Peach Dixie May Rafferty Sutton, will you marry me? I've loved you since the first second I saw you. I promise to love you every second of every day for the rest of my life and to make all your dreams come true. Please marry me."

I lean to kiss his mouth, touching my tongue to his lips. Then I look into his eyes. "I already told you yes."

He slips a ring onto my finger. It's a glinting, flawless yellow diamond, encased in a thick rose gold band. It reminds me of sunshine and peach trees and Georgia summers. "Good. Because the wedding is already planned. For next weekend. It's all arranged. Your grandmother is coming up this weekend to go through some of the final details. And to go shopping. After the wedding we're honeymooning in New Orleans. Just you and me, with no distractions, no hospitals, no customers, no police and no deadlines."

I kiss him again because everything he's saying is music to my ears.

The restaurant is booming and running like clockwork. With my phone and my laptop I can pretty much keep everything running smoothly from wherever I am.

Max didn't end up sending Melanie to prison. But there's a clause. She's on a different kind of house arrest that has one requirement: that she stays away from us for good. If there's any sign of her, she'll be fully prosecuted and sent away for a minimum of five years. Max's bond was refunded in full, all charges were dropped and he was offered his job back. Which he turned down. The app he's building with his developers is getting a lot of press already and is due to launch in a month.

As for me, the judge accepted that I acted in self-defense and for Max's protection and the case was closed.

The stalker's apartment was searched and they found evidence that linked him to more than twenty unsolved criminal cases, some of which were very grisly indeed. It's not hard to guess what probably would have happened to me if the stalker had managed to get me into his van. It's an awful, terrible thought, almost as awful as the realization that I've killed a man. A very bad man, who probably would have gone on to stalk other women, to hurt them and worse. It's good he can't do that anymore. I try not to think about any of that too often. It helps that Max understands what it feels like. Our damages fit together, as it turns out, and help us appreciate what we have, now, maybe even more than we would have. We make the most of every single day.

"So, do you like the apartment?" he says.

"I love it, Max. But we hardly need *five* bedrooms."

"Those are for all the babies we're going to have. Starting whenever you want. Because I'm ready whenever you are."

Max and I get married in the peach orchard of my family's house in Georgia. There are still a few final touches to be done on the grand plantation house but it has almost fully been restored to its former glory. Rafe and Lexi are there, as well as Grandma Bea, Sophie, Johnny and Charlie, Grandma Bea's entourage and a few of my friends from high school and cooking school. Rafe walks me down the aisle to where Max is standing there, looking like a sexy Greek god in his black tux.

We say our vows and he kisses me and kisses me.

After the reception, Grandma Bea takes me and Max aside. "There's somethin' I want to show you two," she says. She hasn't let me see the old cottage at the far end of the peach orchards yet, since it's still being renovated, she said. But she walks us there now.

It has doubled in size. It's white with two gables at the front and a wide front porch that runs the entire length of the cottage. It has a new roof and everything's been painted. There are white roses and purple wisteria vines entwined along the beams and the railings. The view is of the orchards and, beyond them, the rolling hills of Georgia. Gas-lit lanterns cast their soft glow into the dusky night.

"This is for you," Grandma Bea says. "So you'll always have a place of your own here in Georgia. I want ya'll to come visit me a lot. I expect my great grandbabies to be running amok in these orchards within the next few years. So get busy." She directs this last comment at Max. Then she ushers the two of us into the cottage, gives each of us a big hug, and shuts the door, leaving us alone.

The scent of roses and peaches through the open windows is like an elixir for the soul. I wish I could bottle that scent. Then again, I don't need to. Both my homes are filled with it.

It's perfect. The renovations have captured every ounce of the cottage's original charm but the spaces have been expanded and opened up. Everything feels airy and light. There are new, modern appliances, furnishings and decorations. I give Max a tour, amazed at each and every detail as I show it to him. The house is clean and spacious but also cozy and comfortable. It feels like home.

"I guess I better do what Grandma Bea says," Max smiles, and proceeds to carry me to bed, where he lays me down and carefully peels off my designer wedding dress, with its fitted bodice, frayed organza and feather-embroidered full skirt.

"I haven't renewed my prescription," I tell him as he pulls my lace panties off with his teeth.

"What prescription?" he murmurs, kissing a path up my thigh.

"The pill," I breathe.

He stops. His head lifts. "Really?"

"Really."

His dark blue eyes are bright with love and lust. He climbs up my body and unfastens his pants at the same time, shedding his clothes before he lays himself on top of me. His huge cock enters me and I gasp. "Do you want to have a baby with me, Mrs. Black?"

I'm in awe of his glory. "Yes, Mr. Black."

Max pushes my legs apart with his thigh. He kisses me slowly as his cock slides deeper. He takes his time, allowing my body to adjust to him as he thrusts into me. I wrap my legs around him and pull him closer, deeper, clenching my soft core around him as his big body gains momentum, driving harder and deeper. The pleasure begins to spill over. Deep, clenching waves of ecstasy milk the length of him and I can feel the surging throb as he finds his release, flooding me with his silky heat.

We lay like that, his full weight on top of me, my hands curled into his hair as my body adores him, gently rippling around his hot, slippery bulk.

We stare into each other's eyes for a long time as he kisses me endlessly, entwined, bonded, so in love it hurts.

EXACTLY NINE MONTHS later I give birth to twin girls. We name them Rosie and Ruby. They have strawberry-blond curls and blue eyes. My businesses are going exceptionally well. Max thinks I should franchise the bakery, and it's something we might do when we find the time. His app is, so far, one of the most lucrative in history. He takes a cut of each investment made through the game he developed. They've made more money than I can even think about. It turns out I've got a knack for investing, too, as his first customer. Every time I check the numbers I can't believe my eyes. We've started a charity organization whose list of sponsors includes, of all people, Melanie Ames. She contacted us through her lawyer to ask if we were okay with that. She said she wanted to make amends by donating a shitload of money. Last I heard, she's engaged to a hunky but slightly nerdy astrophysicist who thinks she walks on water. Maybe she decided to change her ways.

We divide our time between L.A. and Georgia. The girls do run amok in the peach orchards and I'm teaching them how to roll their dough smoothly and sprinkle it with just the right amount of sugar and cinnamon.

Grandma Bea's house is finished now, restored to well beyond what we ever imagined for it.

Max and I spent our honeymoon in New Orleans, where we held hands as we strolled around the French Quarter, ate gumbo, listened to live music, made love too many times a day to count and drank champagne on a Mississippi river boat. It was fabulous.

Two years after the girls, we have another baby, a boy with red hair and bright blue eyes. We name him Connor Patrick Sutton Black, after my father. He laughs all the time and spends his days climbing peach trees, eating as many as he can get his hands on. That boy has a twinkle in his eye, says Grandma Bea.

A year later, I give birth to our fourth child. We name him Maximillian Apollo Black Junior. He's got dark hair and dark-sapphire eyes like his daddy. He's more brooding and serious-minded than his siblings but, also like his daddy, when he smiles, he lights up the world.

It's late on an August night in Georgia. The children are asleep and the crickets chorus their song outside the open windows. Max is sitting in bed, reading on his laptop. He closes it and sets it aside when I crawl under the covers next to him. I run my fingers along his skin, touching one of his many scars, which almost seem to have faded. He stopped having his nightmares soon after we got married. His newer scar is there, too, the neat round healed-up bullet hole. I kiss each one, like I do every night, then I crawl up his body so I can kiss his lips.

"Thank you for fixing me," he whispers.

"Thank you for making all my dreams come true," I whisper back.

And we live happily ever after.

Thank you for reading! If you enjoyed Max and Peach's story, please consider leaving a quick review or rating on Amazon. Reviews help authors!

Below I've included the first two chapters of **XOXO I Love You**, Rafe and Lexi's story, a super-sexy billionaire romance. Rafe is definitely one of my all-time favorite heroes. If you like OTT alphas who fall hard and fast, you'll love Rafe.

xoxo,

Julie

Please come join my Facebook reader group, Julie

Capulet's Romantics, where I share cover reveals, insider info and we discuss all things romance!

Sign up for my newsletter to receive my free bonus content and get access to sneak peeks and exclusive giveaways!

Visit my website @ www.juliecapulet.com

A young graduate. A ruthless CEO. And an attraction neither of them was prepared for.

Somehow I got an interview at Downtown, the "It" company of the decade.

Sure, I'd heard the rumors about the CEO, Rafe Black. How elusive he was. How rich. How *hot*.

None of it prepared me for what was about to happen. The white-hot lust at first sight. The attraction that wasn't just mutual but obsessive, life-changing and enough to test the limits of what I could handle...

Chapter One

I STEP INTO THE ELEVATOR. And I do my best to ignore how seriously unlikely it is that I'll actually *get* the job I'm about to interview for. I have zero experience, since I only graduated about a month ago. My English degree from Stanford will (hopefully) help, and I graduated (sort of) near the top of my class. But this is *Downtown*, the "It" magazine of the decade. It isn't just a magazine, but a *scene*, with its own fashion label, lifestyle website, pop culture news blog and even a film production company.

My roommate came across the ad for CEO's assistant online only a few days ago. Given the glam factor, it almost seemed strange to stumble across it in a place like that. I would have expected Downtown to recruit from more exotic locations…like in Silicon Valley garages or on French Riviera yachts.

Anyway, I'd applied, and, by some miracle, I actually managed to get an interview. I knew every wannabe in California would be dying to get their résumés seen. Not because we have a lifelong dream to be a CEO's assistant, not at all. But because an underling job like this one might lead to other opportunities within the company—and it's a company every graduate on the planet would sell their teeth to work for. You knew that if you ended up working there, you'd not only rub shoulders with the rich and famous, but also maybe even *become* one of them. They were known for hiring young, hot, über-talented geniuses. Which kind of makes me wonder what *I'm* doing here, but I've decided to just go with it.

As much as I'd like to think I have half a chance, I also know it's definitely a long shot. The email informed me that I'd be meeting with an interview panel. I can picture it now: ten ultra-trendy, over-confident hipsters and one…me.

I take a deep breath.

At least I look the part. As I check out my look in the reflection of the mirrored elevator walls, I can't help but notice that my new makeover has definitely done wonders.

As soon as I arrived in L.A., my roommate Tess dragged me along on a two-day shopping spree and pampering frenzy. Tess runs a make-up and fashion blog that has around fifty thousand followers, so I figured I should probably take her advice. Now, I have a stylish new haircut. I've been massaged, waxed (and I mean *everything*), glossed and groomed to within an inch of my life.

New city, new priorities, according to Tess. *You're no longer a student, you're a hot young urban professional living the dream in the City of Angels.* I'd argued that I wasn't a professional until I actually *landed* a job, but she laughed that detail off as a technicality. *Looking like you do, it's only a matter of time. Employers love hot, and you, my sweet Lexi, are the total package.*

We're about to find out if she's right about any of the above.

I try to let Tess's enthusiasm rub off on me as I stare at my reflection. My long blond hair falls in sleek waves. Highlights of platinum catch the light. Those colorists really know their stuff. My eyelashes have been length-ened by some carefully-applied mascara, also by Tess. A light green silk wrap dress with a short, flouncy skirt hugs my curves and emphasizes the green of my eyes. I wondered if the dress was too fitted and the skirt too short for a job interview, but Tess ordered me to get real. *This is Downtown, honey. They work in bikinis half the time.* Which is true, apparently. She showed me an article about it. Their offices are cutting-edge, modern, ultra-hip and even have pools, swim-up cocktail bars, loungers and tread mill work desks.

To-die-for heeled Miu Miu sandals with feather detailing complete my outfit. The shoes cost a fortune even at seventy percent off, but Tess said I really need to up my fashion game if I want to be taken seriously. I begrudgingly admitted she's right. My wardrobe consists mostly of sweatshirts and jeans—the more comfortable the better, since I've spent the last four years studying 24/7, not to mention the years before that, which were much worse.

Tess also pointed out that my scary new credit card bill will spur my motivation to get earning as quickly as possible. I didn't bother telling her I have that motivation anyway, cringing every time I think of my gargantuan student loan.

Anyway, look out, Downtown, here I come.

The elevator pings and the doors slide open. I enter the lobby. It's all glass and chrome and is positively glimmering with bustle and excitement and glamor. A lone receptionist sits behind a tall desk with a massive print of the L.A. skyline mounted on the wall behind her. There's an etched glass wall next to it that gives a tantalizing glimpse behind the scenes: busy people and racks of designer clothing, desks and film promotion posters. Sliding doors are open, offering views of the pools and palm trees. Music is playing. Everything about it screams *YOU WANT TO WORK HERE*.

The receptionist watches me approach.

"Lexi Blondeau?"

"Yes, hi. I'm scheduled to meet with the interview panel at four thirty."

"Actually, Ms. Blondeau, something came up. You'll be meeting with Mr. Black himself."

Mr. Black.

According to Tess, Rafe Black is famous for his reclusiveness and also his ruthlessness when it comes to business. He's also rumored to be…ridiculously hot. Either way, I'm relieved. A one-on-one meeting sounds a lot less intimidating than a full-blown inquisition.

"He's expecting you," says the receptionist. "Go right on down this hallway. And take the elevator up to the 17th Floor."

The receptionist's phone rings and she points down the white marble hallway before she answers it. I want to ask her what number Mr. Black's office is, but she's already distracted. His door will probably have his name on it, I figure.

Fine, is what I'm thinking. *I can handle this. No problem.* Most likely, he'll be some aloof executive who will run through his list of questions, loftily mutter a we'll-call-you-if-we're-interested dismissal, then send me on my merry way. I already know it's a phone call that'll probably never come. I'll wait a few days before reality sets in, while I meanwhile scour the internet for something slightly more realistic.

I walk down the hallway, and press the button for the elevator. It might be a private elevator. It's not the same one that accesses the lobby of the building.

The elevator swooshes up in that ultra-slick, barely-noticeable way, which gives me vertigo. I reach the 17th floor in about three seconds flat. I teeter unsteadily into a hallway, which has floor to ceiling windows and a killer view of the hazy L.A. skyline, all the way out to the ocean. I take a few seconds to let my equilibrium settle more or less back into place.

So the 17th floor is the *top* floor. There are a couple of swanky leather chairs bathed in sunlight.

Everything is so *luxurious*.

I can't help thinking this would be a perfect place to sit and read a good book while appreciating the view. But of course I'm here for one reason only. To kowtow to the mysterious Rafe Black.

There's only one door. So Mr. Black is the *only* executive with an office on the 17th floor. Well, he *is* the CEO, after all. And the founder of Downtown. And now that I think about it, Tess might have mentioned that he owns at least part of the building. Or maybe the whole thing.

I knock on the door.

And I wait. I check my phone. 4:27.

It might be a full minute before the door opens.

He stands there, wide-legged, silhouetted by the sunlight streaming in from behind him. And—*whoa*—if I was expecting an ordinary, work-addled managerial type, I was sorely mistaken. *Hot* doesn't even begin to cover it. In fact, it takes a few seconds for my eyes to adjust to… just *how* gorgeous Rafe Black actually is.

He's tall, and big. His dark hair is thick and more unruly than you might expect from a CEO. He's wearing an extremely well-cut suit but doesn't seem entirely at ease in it, as though it constricts a barely-controlled wildness that's a definite part of his vibe.

"Mr. Black?" My question comes out breathy and cautious.

His eyes are a deep shade of dark, smoldering blue and have a glint in them that's kind of…electrifying. He assesses me, more than a little cockily. But there's an edge to him, and I get the feeling I've somehow caught him off-guard. He's more tan and rugged-looking than any businessman has a right to be. It wouldn't shock me if he spent most of his time sailing the Southern seas or wrangling bucking broncos in the hot sun. I don't know why I say that. He's got this outdoorsy look, which sort of clashes with the ultra-modern lines of his office and his building. He's too masculine to be called beautiful but it's a word that comes to mind. And it's the kind of over-the-top male beauty that'll hit you…*right there.*

Yikes.

As he opens the door in an invitation for me to enter, his eyes trail intently across my face and my body.

Wow.

This is already…*intense.*

"Ms. Blondeau." His voice is deep, tinged with bass notes that sound almost like a purr. "Please, come in."

I hesitate. Some deep instinct flickers. For a second I wonder if he might be dangerous.

My hesitation seems to amuse him, and he barely cocks his head and scalds me again with those smoky eyes, like he's challenging me. *I dare you.*

The brief, deep-rooted warning is overridden by

something else. A curiosity. A pull that feels more complicated than mere attraction.

What I'm thinking is…*I don't care if he's dangerous.*

I can't quite tear my gaze away from his brawny shoulders and his burly arms, where the muscles are defined even under the layers of his clothing as he clutches the edge of the door with gripping, brutal fingers. As alone as we are, I can't help feeling like I'm walking into Rafe Black's lair. *No one will hear you if you call for help.*

I step into his office and feel a small rush of anxious excitement as he closes the door firmly behind me. *Is it hot in here?* The automatic lock clicks into place. I can feel my heartbeat in strange places.

"You're very punctual, Ms. Blondeau. I like that."

A good start, maybe. "Please. Call me Lexi."

"Lexi." My name, spoken in that molasses-rich voice, sounds strangely erotic. Almost indecent. I find myself wondering what it would sound like…in the dark…as a growl or even a plea as I take his…

What the hell?

I force myself to focus on the reason I'm here: To. Interview. For. A. Job.

This is not like me at all. I'm a clean-cut girl, punctual, reliable to a fault. Socially awkward. And embarrassingly inexperienced. I have never in my life felt such an instant and desperate pull of white-hot lust.

Damn you, Tess! Why did I let her talk me into wearing

such a short, clingy dress? I feel like my clothes are entirely sheer, like Rafe Black is somehow penetrating them with his predatory appraisal as he watches me.

"You found me without too much trouble?"

He's making small talk, to put me at ease, maybe, but I get the feeling that Mr. Black is perceptive, freakishly so, and that he's somehow able to read me very easily. Too easily.

Small talk isn't something I'm good at, but it comes more easily this time, for some reason. "Yes, well, I was glad there was only one door."

He smiles, revealing perfect white teeth.

Holy hell. He really is…very attractive.

"I bought this building specifically for this office," he says. "I prefer total privacy. I like the feeling of being removed from the rest of the world. What do you like, Lexi?"

So he does own the building. "Uh… " *Is he teasing me?* "We had to take personality tests in one of my psychology classes and the results said I'm ninety-three percent intro-vert. So, yes, I can relate."

"We have something in common, then." His eyes do that sparking thing again and…*oh, no…I'm blushing.* "No one can access this floor at any time without my permission."

"Oh." I already know I'm locked in here with him. That no one can get in and that I can't get out unless he *lets* me out. I also know that if I don't *unlock* my eyes from

Rafe Black's sinfully perfect mouth right now, I'm going to do something I'll probably regret.

I find myself desperately hoping my reactions to him aren't somehow…*detectable*. My nipples might barely be visible through the thin silk of my dress, which has a sort of light, built-in bra that might not be fully up to its job. My skin feels warm and flushed, and I'm getting all hot and…*oh, God*…

Flustered, I distract myself by taking in the surroundings. His office is huge. Three walls are windows and the fourth is black marble. There's the elevator and one other steel, space-age-looking door, with blinking electronic locks. A large desk sits in the middle of the room and there's a couch and several leather chairs. One of the glass panes has been folded open, and leads out to a huge patio area and a private pool. Tropical plants and palm trees decorate the space. Everything has clean lines and ultra-swish detailing. Clearly no expense has been spared. The design, at a guess, seems to suggest that Rafe Black is efficient, organized and…controlling. You get the feeling he does things his own way and will tolerate nothing less.

I walk over the window, looking out over the vast expanse of the city, which stretches out toward the distant strip of golden sand and the blue, blue ocean. "You have an amazing view." Okay, not the most ground-breaking observation, but I can congratulate myself on the blithe, offhand tone of my voice, even if it is slightly husked. At least I don't sound as shaken as I feel.

"Come, take a seat." He motions to one of the leather chairs.

I do, as he half-sits against his desk and folds his arms across his chest, causing his suit jacket to tighten against his arms. *Jesus, he's buff. He looks unbelievably strong. If he wanted to, he could so easily overpower me.*

Lexi! I scold myself. *Get a grip right now, girl! He's interviewing you for a dream job, not "overpowering" you!*

I do my best to obey the little voice in my head because I'm still picturing him, *yes…holding me down…pinning me under all that big, hard weight…oh, hell.*

This is bad.

His mouth quirks in a languid half-smile, as though he's reading my thoughts.

Of course he can't. I just need to calm down, and now that I'm sitting, I do. I try to, at least.

But then he takes off his suit jacket and tosses it onto his chair. *Jesus H. Christ.* The man is *ridiculously* built. Tall and muscular, but gracefully so, like a sculpture of a perfect male form. A perfectly *ripped* male form, with toned, hard muscles, as though he's spent the last six months sweatily lifting hay bales in the Outback of Australia or something. As my eyes kind of rove and drink in the sight—don't judge, this guy is seriously freaking hot—I can't help but notice, as much as I try not to, that Rafe Black is impressively built in…well…in *every* conceivable category. There's a sort of…very large…*gigantic, in fact…swell…*

Help me.

"Let's get started," he says.

Yes. Please. I need any distraction I can get at this point.

He reaches for a silver bucket on a stand I hadn't noticed before, behind his desk. He pulls a bottle of champagne out of its bucket of ice. "This might seem a little strange, but this bottle was delivered only a few minutes before you arrived. It's from my brother, Max."

"Oh. Are you celebrating something?"

"Today's my birthday."

"Happy birthday."

"Thank you," he says. "Can I tempt you?"

I can't even begin to describe how tempted I am. I know I probably shouldn't accept his offer. A glass of champagne will only annihilate my self-control, which at this point I badly need. But I can hardly say no. It's his *birthday.* "Thank you."

He smiles, and his gaze lingers on my mouth, before returning to my eyes. That brief, subtle glance has all the effect of a shot of pure, uncut aphrodisiac.

No one should be this good-looking. Or this much of a big, rugged, sexy tomcat. All I can think of is hot, sweaty, down-and-dirty sex—which I have absolutely zero experience with whatsoever—and it's freaking me out. I really have no idea what's come over me. "There's no reason we can't enjoy my brother's gift while we get down to business."

Rafe Black pours two glasses of champagne and hands one to me.

Then he sits in the chair that's next to mine. He looks even bigger this close. And even more manly and mouth-watering, if that's possible.

I could reach out and touch him…it would be that easy.

What would he do? Would he let me?

Somehow, I know he would.

His eyes blaze and I get that feeling again that he's able to read me—if not my thoughts, then…my vibes. With chemistry *this* off-charts, it wouldn't surprise me. I'm finding it a little hard to breathe with him this close to me.

"As you know," he says, "I'm looking for a new assistant. I've had the same assistant since I founded the company seven years ago. She's sort of a Moneypenny type. She's retiring."

"You must have been young when you founded Downtown, Mr. Black." I wonder if he's even thirty. He looks younger than that.

"Call me Rafe." His wicked mouth quirks. He's a rich, powerful mogul, obviously. And I'm an unemployed, entry-level nobody. I am, in more ways than one, at his mercy. His request for me to call him by his first name feels like a small triumph. A connection. An invitation for familiarity that's ridiculously enticing.

"Rafe," I repeat. The name suits him. Strong, dark, commanding.

His eyes are intense, and I get the feeling that something about the way I've said his name has affected him. "I was twenty. Still at Stanford."

"I also went to Stanford."

"I saw that on your résumé. It was one of the reasons I decided to interview you." I wonder what the other reasons are, but I hold my questions. Maybe it's best if he does the talking. My nerves have made me thirsty, and the champagne is the most delicious I've ever had. I sip again.

"Are you aware that Downtown is only one of the companies I own?" he says. "One of the smaller ones, in fact."

"I didn't know that."

"We run the magazine and all its off-shoots, as well as several hedge funds, an investment company and a real estate brokerage firm."

I'm beginning to grasp just how rich and powerful Rafe Black actually is.

"I have to be honest," I tell him. "I've never been an assistant before. I did an internship last summer for a literary agency. The job mainly involved reading manu-scripts and writing up reports. But I'm a quick learner and a hard worker. And very eager to please."

His eyes spangle, and I realize what that must have sounded like. *What's wrong with me? Why the hell did I just say that?* I blush again.

"I'm very glad to hear that," is his soft reply. "I think your résumé and references speak for themselves." His long fingers curl around the stem of his champagne glass.

He looks like he could easily snap it without any effort at all. His eyes burn as he takes another sip. "I'm impressed."

I think I might be combusting inside this potent cloud of alpha-male pheromones he's emitting. My senses are hyper-aware, and my body feels unsettlingly warm…*and soft…and—oh, hell, this is way too much…*

Rafe rubs his hand across his jaw. He's so freaking… *sexy*…it's overwhelming me. His cinnamon skin, the stubble of his beard. *I can just tell it'll be rough and might even hurt a little.* His mouth, his thick hair, his dark blue eyes rimmed with thick black lashes. The man is an absolute specimen of hot sin and alpha male energy. And let's be clear about one thing: I'm not usually the type of girl who goes around thinking about alpha male energy *or* hot sin. Until now, apparently. "I do require that whoever I hire must be available immediately."

"I'm available whenever you want me." *Oops.* I realize the double entendre only *after* I make the comment, of course. Clearly my brain has turned to mush. My cheeks burn. "I meant, of course, that I'm available whenever you decide you'd, um, like me to start, *if* you want to hire me, that is."

"It's a demanding job. Long hours. I need someone who can basically be at my beck and call, at any hour of the day or night. We have affiliates in New York, London, Paris, Sydney, and so on, so we're a 24-hour business. It can be hard on…significant others, if you were to be working a lot."

"I don't have a significant other. I have a roommate, but she's busy most of the time, building her business."

"Good," he says, and his smug charisma hits me in the low pit of my stomach. God, he's so freaking cocky. *And it's doing things to me I can't even begin to describe.* "There will be times when you'll be required to travel with me. Frequently, in fact. Do you like to travel?"

"I haven't really had much opportunity to travel." I don't tell him that I never had the money. Or, that as a graduation present to myself, I decided to get my passport issued. Or, that it had just been delivered in the mail. Last week, in fact. "But I've always wanted to."

"Perfect." Rafe tops up our glasses. Then he reaches for a pen and a small piece of paper. He scrawls some numbers onto the paper and hands it to me. "This is the starting salary. Negotiable, of course. I'll cover all business-related expenses. You'll have a driver, and an expense account, if you agree to take the position. In addition, my apartment is in this building, and I have an adjoining studio apartment available for your use, if you have need of it from time to time, which you will, when I require you to work late."

I glance at the number he's written and hold back a gasp, wondering if my eyes are deceiving me. It's more than triple what I might have expected to earn from an assistant's job. A salary this generous will allow me to pay off my student loan within two years, especially if I can cut down on other expenses. Which I'll clearly be able to do, with all that he's offering me.

"What do you say, Lexi?"

"I say…yes. This is absolutely my dream job. Thank you so much, Mr.—"

"Rafe."

His black-satin voice seems to penetrate the air as a physical force, touching me and ruffling me. *How does he do that?* "Rafe."

He smiles. "It's settled, then."

This is happening so fast. I can't believe I just got *hired*. By *Downtown*. More specifically, by its drop-dead gorgeous CEO.

Rafe places his glass on the table and leans in his chair. As he moves, I catch a light whiff of his scent. He smells of soap and mint and raw masculinity. And there's more to it. Something elusive and outrageously, crazily appealing. The light-musked spice unfurls something in me, intoxicating me along with the champagne. My nerves are gone now, replaced by…sweet, soft, brimming heat. I feel reckless and a little crazy, if you really want to know.

My eyes rove down his long, powerful body and—*holy hell*. It's obvious that he's getting as worked up as I am. *His…the front of his pants…is straining…unbelievably…almost like it might…bust out…*

I can't handle this.

What would it feel *like?*

Lexi. Stop. Right now. Seriously. "When…w-would you like me to start?"

"How about right now?"

Our gazes meet. I'm having trouble breathing in enough air. I want to breath *his* air, his breath. That scent of him, that one hit, was not enough.

He leans closer. His dark eyes are burning with some unfathomable emotion.

Then, his hand lifts, brushing against an end strand of my hair.

He's touching me.

His fingers twirl around a soft lock of my hair, forming a lightly ensnaring hold. Very gently, he pulls.

I follow his pull. My self-control has been obliterated. I want this job, but even more, I want *him*. Sensing my consent, he pulls me closer, and closer, until my mouth is close to his. My nipples peak into tight little buds of sensation. Concentrated lust seemed to center there, and radiates slowly through my body in shimmery, uninhibited waves.

His lower lip is close to my mouth, as plump as ripe fruit. I'm high from his effect, and so desperate for more of that scent and the *taste* of him, I can't control it. This lust. This craving. It's bigger than me.

"Lexi." The whispered word is so dark, so deep. "I wasn't expecting—" He stops, his breathing heavier, as though he's conflicted.

I have no idea what's happening to me, but whatever it is, it's profound. I'm falling. That's the only way to describe it. I can't stop it. And I don't want to.

When his mouth brushes against my lips in a feather-light kiss that promises so much more, I touch my tongue to the rounded curve of his lip. He groans, and his fingers graze my nipple through the soft fabric of my dress. He teases it between his thumb and fingers, kneading it into a ripe bud. Searing sensation surges through my body.

Oh my God. This is really happening.

I gasp as he pinches tighter, rolling my aching flesh more insistently, controlling me entirely with his touch.

"*Lexi,*" he says again, against my mouth. He cups my breast in his warm palm, squeezing lightly. "*Fuck.*"

I get what he means. The ferocious urges of my body are driving me, and I realize with a tiny shred of concern that's swept away by an ocean of surrender that I'll do anything he asks. Anything. His effect is flooding me with fire.

He pulls at the knot of my dress, untying it. The fabric falls open to reveal my breasts. They feel full and soft. The rosy hue of my swollen nipples looks almost—and this isn't something I'd usually stop to consider—*sultry* against the pale white of my skin. I feel more beautiful than I've ever felt in my life. Because of him and the way he's looking at me. Like he wants to eat me alive.

Rafe makes a soft, savage sound. He seems overcome. He's torn, I can see, by the thought of taking advantage of me, his new, young assistant, if he'll even hire me now. It's a strange and sudden turn of events, and completely unexpected. But I'm too far gone to allow his internal dilemma to steal from me this stunningly needy anticipation. I don't care. I want him.

"Lexi. Do you want this?" His voice is low and deep and so appealing it pushes me past some barrier of self-control. "Tell me to stop and I will."

No. Don't stop. No stopping…

Very lightly, I brush my lips against his again. As soon as I do, his tongue sinks into my mouth, hungrily, filling my entire being with want. I suck on his tongue, gently greedy, desperate to take more of any part of his body into mine.

"*Lexi.* Fucking hell. You taste so damn good." His voice has become rasped with lust and…not indecision, but turmoil over a decision already made.

I want more from this beautiful, god-like *beast* than I've ever wanted anything in my life. He pulls me closer to him and I stand up. His gaze rakes sort of…*adoringly* over my body.

"You're so *beautiful.*" He sounds awed. Just like that, like I'm already his, he pulls off my dress, so all I'm wearing is my panties and my heeled sandals.

I feel like I've just climbed out of some underwater seashell and been reborn as a lusty nymph who has no inhibitions, who's made purely of hot, wet physical sensation. I know the thin, clinging fabric of my panties is revealing to him…pretty much everything.

Rafe's dark eyes are heavy-lidded as he reaches slowly to slide his thumb across the saturated silk. I gasp because it feels *so good*. He licks his lips. "You're so wet for me, baby. I want to see you."

Rafe Black clearly isn't into second guessing things, because he rips my panties, with hardly any effort at all, tossing the tiny shred of fabric away.

This is happening. This is going *to happen.*

At the thought, I feel happier than maybe I ever have in my life.

"Lexi. Jesus Christ. You're *unbelievably* fucking gorgeous."

A hint of shyness—some vanishing piece of my old self—loosens. I *want* him to see me. It's beyond crazy, but I want to entice him.

I'm standing between his knees. My breasts are close to his mouth. He takes them in his big, warm hands, plumping them to his mouth. Watching my eyes, he eases his hungry mouth around one of my nipples, licking and sucking in lusty pulls.

Oh my God.

I moan. It's too *good*, too rife with sensation. Each tug sends a wash of molten feeling deeper, lower. I feel unbearably hot and ripe, *there*, like I've been dipped in warm honey. I feel like I might…be close to the edge. Already.

His strong hands clamp onto my hips—*and holy hell, he's strong*—pulling me onto his lap, holding me exactly where he wants me. Our eyes lock in a connective link. A strand of his black hair has fallen over his forehead, somehow softening his severe beauty. I touch the thick silk of it, as our gazes hold, and a startling thread of tenderness passes between us, strengthening the lust, stoking it. "You're so damn sweet," he murmurs.

Tentatively, because I have never, ever done anything like this before, I ease my palm over the massive ridge of his hard-on. It's stunningly hard, and hot, even through the layer of his clothing. I try to unzip him, fumbling with the fastenings, too hazed in a trancelike eagerness. He helps me and I gasp when he's fully revealed to me. At the sheer size and perfection of him.

I touch him tenderly, taking his hot length in my hands, exploring and feathering with my fingertips. "*Oh, fuck,*" he groans. A bead of moisture seeps out of the tip of his cock. *Is he about to…?* I'm completely new at this and have no idea what to expect. I touch my fingers to him, swirling the wetness it until he's slippery.

Rafe's hand takes mine. "I'm going to come if you keep doing that, honey. Come here."

Rafe pulls me onto him and positions me so I'm straddling his hips. Then he begins to move me, closer, until—*oh, God*—he's touching me. *There.* I let him move me along his length, until his cock is slick with my own juices. Rafe's thumb circles, centering, skating over the tiny nub, which feels electric and hyper-sensitive, igniting a sweet, slow swell. If he does that again, I'll lose it completely.

Instead, he guides the broad tip of his cock to my snug, slippery entrance, easing the head of his cock barely inside me. It's too much. *Feeling* him there. The pleasure is unbearable. My orgasm starts slowly. I'm riding some sort of precipice. My inner muscles flutter around him, drawing him deeper. "*Lexi. Oh, baby.*" Then he grasps my hips in a firm grip and, using the rhythm of my own body, pushes into me. I'm too tight, but the wetness and his thrusting drives force his thickness deeper. And deeper. His fingers glide over my clit, and the pleasure explodes in a rich, crazy rush. It feels excruciatingly good. I feel blinded with it. Needy and totally overcome. Each ripple of my orgasm pulls him deeper and we move together, grinding, needing more, until I'm fully impaled, riding the huge, thick length of him. His bold fingers work a soft rhythm, spinning my climax further, deeper, higher. Aware of nothing but the astounding pleasure, my body grips him tightly, and he groans like he's in pain. He's saying something but I can't comprehend it. *Wait. You're too beautiful. I can't hold on.* But my body is too possessive, too slippery. I'm riding him, pulling him deeper. I feel the flooding wetness, the thick, hot pulse of him deep inside me. The silky jets of his climax take me over another edge, the rush of spiraling waves milking him softly, again and again.

Oh.

Wow.

Just wow.

I'm floating.

I think I might be in love.

Is it possible to fall in love this fast?

With a complete and total stranger?

We stay there for a long time, rocked by the intensity of what just happened. Of what's *still* happening. Rafe's burly arms are wrapped tightly around me. He's still deep inside me. My head rests on his hard chest. I can hear his heart beating.

I'm fully aware that, only a few short hours ago, I would have been shocked by my total abandon. I barely recognize myself. The consequence of what we've just done can—and probably will—be far-reaching, but I feel surprisingly removed from any of that. All I am is this moment. I feel supremely, ridiculously peaceful. I'm warm, and euphoric, cocooned in this haven high above the bustling city, wrapped in the arms and still wetly connected to a total (and unbelievably beautiful) stranger. I don't want to move. I don't want to break this bubble of bliss that, even now, holds on.

I don't know why I abandoned every sane, reasonable thought to get as close as possible to Rafe Black. All I know is that he's mine. I want to keep him. And I'll do it all over again if he'll let me.

It doesn't make sense, but that's just the way it is.

After a while, I move a little. With the small change in

position, Rafe's barely-softened cock slides deeper inside me. I'm a little surprised that he's still as big—and *hard*—as he is. I have no experience with these things, but I think this might be kind of unusual. In a subtle adjustment, he moves me, causing his cock to swell even deeper in a vague, circular rub that triggers—*oh, God*—a new, instant heat. I'm not sure how I can be so easily turned on—*again*—and so soon after what we've just done. He obviously feels the same way. He doesn't care about reason, just *this*. It's too powerful. *It's too insanely good.*

It seems amazing to me that he's still almost fully clothed. I want to get closer. I unbutton the top buttons of his shirt, breathing in his masculine scent, layered now with sweat and musk and lust. I touch my tongue to his skin. He's salty and mouth-watering.

"Kiss me," he says. "Give me your mouth."

I do, and he dips his tongue into me in a synced rhythm as he thrusts his big cock deeper.

He hugs me against his body, gripping me and easily lifting me. Still deep inside me, he lays me onto his desk. His messed-up hair frames his heart-breaking face. I *love* this: the cool, unapproachable top-floor CEO turned untamed, beefed-up sex god. His dark blue eyes glimmer and his gaze is tender under his lust. He kisses me again, like he can't get enough.

He grips me with both hands, lifting my hips higher so he can slide even deeper. It hurts a little. He's so freaking *big* and thick and *deep*. It's like he's fully occupying every-thing about me.

He slows his movements. He's listening to me, gauging every breath, every whimper. I'm not sure if I can come again, but his drives are measured and relent-less. Rafe is reading my reactions as he plays my body, taking every quivering flutter to heart. With unequivocal insistence, he coaxes a rising surge. "Come for me, baby. I love the little sounds you make. Come for me, gorgeous Lexi. My gorgeous girl."

"*Rafe,*" I moan, as his thick length rubs against a ridiculously sensitive trigger inside me.

Cocky, he pushes the pleasure deeper. I ride the tidal wave, shattering. I dig my nails into his back, as my inner muscles work his own orgasm with long, tight, silky pulls. He doesn't try to pull out this time, and I don't ask him to. It hardly seems to matter. We're already bound.

You've totally lost your mind.

Yes. And there's not a damn thing I—or you—can do about it.

After the waves calm, Rafe strokes my hair for a while. He kisses my face. Then he pulls gently out of me. He stands above me, all hulking and outrageous. Then, abruptly, he pauses, touching his fingers to my body. He looks appalled, almost furious, as he stares at his blood-stained fingers.

"Lexi. My God. You're a *virgin?*"

Chapter Two

RAFE

Fuck.

I can't believe I got so ridiculously carried away. *Christ. I just fucked my new assistant.*

The new assistant who's still peacefully sleeping in my bed with me.

I meant to pull out, at least. But I was so fucking over-come with lust that I spent myself inside her. More than once. There was simply no way in hell I could have disengaged myself from that tight little heaven on earth.

Goddamn it all to hell. That has never, ever happened before. Not even close. It didn't even *occur* to me to put on a condom. Or anything else. The minute that goddess walked into my office, with her sultry green eyes and her short skirt, practically oozing sexuality, my brain took flight and left the room. Leaving my goddamn cock in charge, which was never a good thing.

She's so fucking *young*, with a pronounced vibe of complete and total innocence.

The sane part of my mind wants to wake her, to politely ask her to leave, to tell her I still have a few more people to interview and I'll be in touch. I won't call. I'll send her some flowers and a gentlemanly note. Done and dusted. She's not the most qualified for the job anyway, not by a long shot.

I watch her as she sleeps, surprised at myself for even bringing her here. I never bring women to my apartment. It's a door I keep decisively closed. Until now, apparently.

Her sunny blond hair spills over the pillow in a silky cascade. Her pink lips are puffy from my greedy kisses, absurdly soft and tempting. The smooth skin of her jaw is reddened slightly from the stubble of my beard. I was rough with her. Too rough. I took her not only in my office—twice—but several times during the night, damning all consequences. And she's a fucking *virgin*.

Or at least she was. Yesterday.

She must be twenty-one at least. Maybe twenty-two. What kind of girl waits that long? And why?

Her dark-blond eyelashes lay in graceful curves against her pale cheeks, dark at the roots and lightening to an almost white-blond at the tips. Her make-up is all but gone, aside from some light smudges on the pillow-case. I think of waking her, just so I can see that sea-green burn in her eyes.

The sheet lays low on her hips, drawing a line across the concave plane of her stomach, framed by the jut of her angular hipbones. Her breasts are a work of art—there's no other way to describe them. Full and rounded, high and plush with youth. Her nipples are soft now, in sleep. And I can't resist. I'm already harder than I'd ever been. Maybe equal to yesterday, or last night. I hardly care about the comparison. What I care about is the soft bud of her rosy skin, tightening even as she sleeps, under the glide of my tongue. She tastes like nothing I've ever experienced. Sweet, somehow. Floral. Like she stepped out of a garden at midnight, while eating sugary cake and blossoming into full-blown womanhood. I suck on her like I'm trying to draw that taste from her body. It's perverse, almost, the greed and need I feel.

Little moans of pleasure come from her mouth. She writhes under the sheet, displacing it.

Fuck.

I'm a fucking goner. I'm whipped like nothing I've ever known. Just the sight of her is enough to blind me, once again, to every normal consideration. I've been a high-achieving, successful, responsible, Type-A paramour, sometimes more darkly than others, all my life. Every fucking second of my entire straight-A millionaire—actually, as of last month, *billionaire*—life.

But *this*. This *girl*. She disarms me. She makes me want to fuck everything up. I want to dirty myself, and her. Now I know what it feels like to not care about anything but the moment, because *this* moment will be so good, so incomparably fucking good that nothing else matters.

I lick my way down her body, but I don't linger. I'm too frantic. Too needy. I let my tongue delve into her soft-ness. Her willingness only compounds this overblown, excessive desire. Her hands are in my hair and she's lifting herself to my mouth, pulling me closer. I play her with my tongue, easing two fingers inside her. I wait for her to relax into the invasion. I know she's sore. I try to be gentle.

I wait for her to come to me, to beg for more. Gently, I zero in on the tender bud, licking and sucking her in soft pulls. Her moans and the clutch of her hands in my hair are driving me mad, but I remind myself who I am. A control freak. A successful, driven, disciplined man. A few soft moans of a willing woman should hardly undo me. But then it begins. Her hips sway in a back-and-forth rhythm. She cries out my name.

I'm mildly appalled with myself, with my reaction, how much I *love* that sound. Of her, calling to me. Saying my name in that dreamy exhale, like I'm some mythical god she can't believe. Like I'm too good to be true.

I'm about to come whether I'm inside her or not. And there's no question I'll take her, fuck her, make love to her. The semantics hardly matter. All I know is that there's nothing more sacred to me at this moment than being inside her. Her climax is starting. She's starting to spasm as I slide my raging cock deep, driving into her and compounding her pleasure. If I cared about proving myself, of prolonging and lasting, the concern at that moment is inconsequential. That snug, pulsing embrace is so tight, so insistent, all my restraint is pulled from my body in silky, furtive tugs that leave me no choice. This is ecstasy in its purest form. The release is complete and total. I fall willingly, succumbing entirely to the perfect bliss of her, beautiful as sin, absolute as death.

It takes me a while to return to myself.

I can't think. I can only *feel.*

One thing I know: this is bad.

Very, very bad.

This girl.

I've found my weakness.

And I am utterly, hopelessly addicted.

ALSO BY JULIE CAPULET

I Love You Series

The Obsession Begins (free)

XOXO I Love You

XOXX I Love You More

Love You The Most (free)

Sexy Standalones

Max

Cowboy

McCabe Brothers Series

Hopeless Romantic

My Hero

Arrogant Player

Music City Lovers Series

Nashville Days

Nashville Nights

Nashville Dreams

Nashville Lights

Hawthorne U Series

Lovestruck

Paradise Series

Devil's Angel

Wild Hearts

New York Billionaires Series

Billionaire Boss

Billionaire Grump

Billionaire Devil

Billionaire Romantic

Standalone Rom-com

Beautiful Savages

ABOUT THE AUTHOR

Julie Capulet is an Amazon top 20 bestselling author of contemporary romance. She writes steamy he-falls-first romance with heart, heat and fairy tale HEAs. Her stories are inspired by true love and she's married to her own real life hero. When she's not writing, she's reading, traveling, walking on the beach and watching rom-coms.

www.juliecapulet.com

9 781968 790080